"Why Didn't You Tell Me When You Found Out You Were Pregnant?"

It was the question Jessica had been dreading ever since she'd made the decision not to tell him.

It had been the wrong decision. Or at the very least, the wrong thing to do. There had been so many factors to consider, though, and she'd been so very frightened and alone.

To Alex, however, she said simply, "I didn't think you'd want to know. Most men wouldn't."

"I'm not most men," he said slowly and very deliberately, almost as though each word was a statement unto itself. "I would have stepped up to the plate. And I most certainly would have wanted to know I'd fathered a child."

"I'm sorry."

Jessica didn't know what else ___ ___ ___ ithout saying far too much.

Dear Reader,

I am absolutely delighted to share *Secrets, Lies & Lullabies* with you because…well, here's a little secret of my own— this story has been playing at the back of my mind for quite some time. It's actually an idea I first began working on several years ago. Which is proof, I guess, that one should never give up on an idea one feels strongly about, even if it has to be set aside for a while to focus on other things.

A bit of replotting and a lot of rewriting were required, but I'm finally able (and delighted!) to share Alex and Jessica and their passionate romance with you. It has a little of everything, too—a torrid affair, an attempt at revenge, a secret baby and definitely a happily-ever-after.

I hope you enjoy!

Heidi Betts

HeidiBetts.com

HEIDI BETTS

SECRETS, LIES & LULLABIES

HARLEQUIN®
entertain, enrich, inspire™

Recycling programs
for this product may
not exist in your area.

ISBN-13: 978-0-373-73206-7

SECRETS, LIES & LULLABIES

Copyright © 2012 by Heidi Betts

Printed in U.S.A.

HEIDI BETTS

An avid romance reader since junior high, *USA TODAY* bestselling author Heidi Betts knew early on that she wanted to write these wonderful stories of love and adventure. It wasn't until her freshman year of college, however, when she spent the entire night before finals reading a romance novel instead of studying, that she decided to take the road less traveled and follow her dream.

Soon after Heidi joined Romance Writers of America, her writing began to garner attention, including placing in the esteemed Golden Heart competition three years in a row. The recipient of numerous awards and stellar reviews, Heidi's books combine believable characters with compelling plotlines, and are consistently described as "delightful," "sizzling" and "wonderfully witty."

For news, fun and information about upcoming books, be sure to visit Heidi online at HeidiBetts.com.

To Rob and Michelle (Timko) Massung,
for all of their amazing computer help recently.
You saved my butt more than you will ever know,
and I just can't thank you enough.

One

Alexander Bajoran swiped his key card and pushed open the heavy oak door to his suite. He'd been halfway down the winding mile-long drive leading away from the luxurious yet rustic resort—aptly named Mountain View Lodge—when he realized he'd forgotten a stack of much-needed paperwork. Now he was late for his meeting, and it was going to be nearly impossible to make it into downtown Portland on time.

He let the door swing closed behind him as he marched toward the large cherrywood desk on the far side of the sitting area. Six steps in, he stopped short at the sound of someone else moving around in the suite. Turning toward the bedroom, he paused in the doorway, taking note of the woman stripping his bed and shaking her rear end to a song only she could hear.

She was wearing a maid's uniform, but sadly not one of the sexy French variety. Just a simple gray dress that did nothing to compliment her figure or coloring.

Her blond hair was pulled up and twisted at the back of her head, held in place by a large plastic clip, but he could still see bits of color peeking out here or there. A thin streak of black, then auburn, then blue running down one side and blending into the rest.

Yes, blue. The woman had blue hair. At least a few bits of it.

She was humming beneath her breath, the occasional odd lyric tripping off her tongue as she whipped back the top sheet, then a corner of the fitted one. The quilted coverlet was already in a heap on the floor.

As she danced around, oblivious to his presence, he noticed the glitter of earrings lining the entire length of one ear. Studs, hoops, dangles; there must have been seven or eight in her right ear alone. The left had only four that he could see—three near the lobe and one higher up near her temple.

Despite all the silver and gold and jeweled settings, he knew they had to be fake. No way could a chambermaid afford the real thing. Which was a shame, because she'd look good in diamonds. And he should know—diamonds were his business.

Soiled sheets balled up in her arms, she turned suddenly, jumping back and giving a high-pitched shriek when she saw him standing there.

He held his hands up in the universal I-mean-you-no-harm gesture. "I didn't mean to startle you," he offered by way of apology.

Reaching up, she yanked the buds from her ears and tucked them into the pocket of the white apron that must have held her MP3 player. He could hear the heavy beat of her music as she fumbled to turn down the volume.

Now that he could look at her straight on, he noticed she wasn't wearing makeup…or not much, at any rate. Strange, considering her hair and jewelry choices. She even had a small gold hoop with a tiny fleck of cubic zirconia hanging from the outer edge of her right eyebrow.

Eyes still wide from the scare he'd given her, she licked her lips. "I'm sorry, I didn't know anybody would be here. I didn't see the sign on the knob."

He shook his head. "There wasn't one. I expected to be gone for the day, but forgot something I need for a meeting."

He didn't know why he was telling her this. He didn't normally spend a lot of time explaining himself to anyone. But the longer he stood here talking, the longer he got to look at her. And he did enjoy looking at her.

That, too, was unusual for him. The women he dated tended to be socialites from wealthy families. Polished and sophisticated, the type who spent their days at the garden club doing nothing more strenuous than planning their next thousand-dollar-a-plate fundraiser for the charity du jour.

Never before had he found himself even remotely attracted to someone with multicolored hair and excessive piercings. But the young woman standing in front of him was fascinating in an exotic-animal, priceless-piece-of-artwork way.

She seemed to be slightly disconcerted by his presence, as well, staring at him as if she expected him to bite.

"Is there anything you need, as long as I'm here?" she asked, nervously licking her lips over and over again. "Extra towels or glasses, that sort of thing?"

He shook his head. "I'm fine, thank you."

Then, because he couldn't think of anything else to say or any other reason to stand there, staring at the help as though she was on display, he moved away, heading back across the sitting room and grabbing up the file he'd forgotten. It was her turn to stand in the bedroom doorway while he slapped the manila folder against his free hand a couple of times.

"Well," he murmured, for no particular reason, "I'll leave you to it, then."

She inclined her head in acknowledgment, still watching him warily.

Walking to the suite's main door, he pulled it open and set one foot across the threshold into the hall. But before walking off, he couldn't resist turning back and taking one last glance at the intriguing young woman who had already returned to her job of changing his sheets.

"It was Alexander Bajoran," Jessica said in a harsh whisper, leaning so far across the small round deli table that her nose very nearly touched her cousin's.

"You're kidding," Erin returned in an equally hushed voice, her eyes going wide in amazement.

Jessica shook her head, crossed her arms over her chest and flopped back in her chair, causing her cousin to move forward in hers. Their sandwiches sat untouched in front of them, their ice-filled fountain drinks slowly producing rivulets of condensation down the sides of the paper cups.

"Did he recognize you?" Erin asked.

"I don't know. He didn't say anything, but he *was* looking at me a little funny."

"Funny, how?"

Jessica flashed her a tiny grin. "The usual."

"Well, you do tend to stand out."

Jessica stuck her tongue out at her cousin's teasing. "We can't all be prim and proper Jackie O wannabes."

"Nobody's asking you to be Jackie O. The family just wishes you weren't quite so intent on being the next Courtney Love."

Following through on the natural instincts that had probably earned her that reputation in the first place, Jessica flipped her cousin a good-natured hand gesture. Not the least offended by the response, Erin merely rolled her eyes.

"Actually, your unique personal style may work in our

favor. You don't look at all the way you did five years ago. Chances are, Bajoran won't have a clue who you are."

"I hope not. I'll try to switch floors with Hilda, though. That should keep me from accidentally bumping into him again."

"No, don't do that!" Erin said quickly. "The fact that he doesn't recognize you is a good thing. You can move around his suite freely without arousing suspicion."

"Arousing suspicion?" Jessica repeated. "Who am I— James Bond?"

"If I could do it, I would, believe me," Erin told her with no small amount of bitterness leeching into her voice. "But you're the one he already thinks is a chambermaid."

Jessica narrowed her eyes. "Why does that matter?"

"Because it means you can move around the lodge without being noticed. You know what men like Bajoran are like. Rich and self-absorbed…to him, you'll be all but invisible."

Jessica understood her cousin's anger, really she did. Fifty years ago, Alexander Bajoran's grandfather and great-uncle had launched Bajoran Designs. Soon after, they'd begun a partnership with Jessica's and Erin's grandfathers, who owned Taylor Fine Jewels. Both companies had been based in Seattle, Washington, and together they'd been responsible for creating some of the most beautiful and valuable jewelry in the world. Million-dollar necklaces, bracelets and earrings worn by celebrities and royalty across the globe.

The Taylor-Bajoran partnership had lasted for decades, making both families extremely wealthy. And then one day about five years ago, Alexander had taken over Bajoran Designs from his father, and his first order of business had been to steal *her* family's company right out from under them.

Without warning he'd bought up a majority of shares of Taylor Fine Jewels and forced Jessica's and Erin's fathers off the Board of Directors so he could absorb the company into his own and essentially corner the market on priceless jewels and their settings.

Thanks to Alexander's treacherous move, the Taylor family had gone bankrupt and been driven out of Seattle almost overnight. They were far from destitute, but all the same, the Taylors were *not* used to living frugally. Jessica didn't think her mother was used to her new, more middle-class lifestyle even now, and Erin's mother had taken the reversal of fortune hardest of all.

Jessica was doing okay, though. Did she *enjoy* being a maid at a resort where she used to be a guest? Where she used to stay in a three-thousand-dollar-a-night suite and that her family could easily have purchased with a flick of the wrist?

Not always. But being a maid, working at a normal job like a normal person, gave her a freedom she'd never felt as a rich, well-known socialite. No way could she have gotten away with streaks in her hair and pierced everything when she'd been one of *those* Taylors. When she'd been attending luncheons at the country club with her mother and been the subject of regular snapshots by local and national paparazzi.

Money was good, but she thought anonymity might be a little bit better. For her, at least. For Erin, she knew the opposite was true.

"Why do I need to be invisible?" she asked finally. "It's lucky enough he didn't recognize me the first time. I should switch floors and maybe even shifts with one of the other girls before he does."

"No!" Erin exploded again. "Don't you see? This is our chance! Our chance to get back at that bastard for what he did to us."

"What are you talking about?" Thoroughly confused, Jessica shook her head. "How could we possibly get back at him for that? He's a millionaire. Billionaire. The CEO of a zillion-dollar company. We're nobodies. No money, no power, no leverage."

"That's right, we're nobodies. And he's the CEO of a zillion-dollar company that *used* to be ours. Maybe it could be again."

Before Jessica had the chance to respond, Erin rushed on. "He's here on business, right? That means he has to have business information with him. Paperwork, contracts, documents we could use to possibly get Taylor Fine Jewels back."

"Taylor Fine Jewels doesn't exist anymore. It's been absorbed into Bajoran Designs."

"So?" Erin replied with a shrug of one delicate shoulder. "It can always be un-absorbed."

Jessica didn't know how that would work. She wasn't sure it was even possible. But whether it was or it wasn't, what Erin was suggesting was insanity.

"I can't go poking around in his things. It's wrong. And dangerous. And corporate espionage. And *definitely* against Mountain View policy. I could lose my job!"

Her cousin made a sound low in her throat. "It's only corporate espionage if you're employed by a rival company. Which you're not, because Alexander Bajoran *stole* our company and put us all out on the street. And who cares if you lose that stupid job? Surely you can scrub toilets for the wealthy elite at some other high-priced hotel."

Jessica leaned back, stunned by the venom in her cousin's voice, as well as her obvious disdain for Jessica's occupation. Yes, she scrubbed toilets and stripped beds and vacuumed carpets instead of folding scarves and dressing mannequins at an upscale boutique like Erin, but she kind of liked it. She got to spend most of her time alone, got along well with the rest of the housekeeping staff and didn't have to claim her sometimes quite generous tips on her taxes.

And it kept her busy enough that she didn't have time to

dwell on the past or nurse a redwood-size grudge against an old enemy the way her cousin obviously did.

"Come on, Jess. Please," Erin begged. "You have to do this. For the family. We may never get another opportunity to find out what Bajoran is up to, or if there's some way— *any way*—to rebuild the business and our lives."

She wanted to refuse. *Should* refuse. But the pain in Erin's voice and in her eyes gave Jessica pause.

She could maybe poke around a little.

"What would I have to do?" she asked carefully. "What would I be looking for?"

"Just…see if you can find some paperwork. On the desk, in his briefcase if he leaves it. Interoffice memos, maybe, or documents outlining his next top secret, underhanded take-over."

Against her better judgment, Jessica gave a reluctant nod. "All right, I'll do it. But I'm not going to get caught. I'll *glance around.* Keep my eyes open. But I'm not going to rummage through his belongings like a common thief."

Erin's nod was much more exuberant. "Fine, I understand. Just look around. Maybe linger over fluffing the pillows if he's on the phone…listen in on his conversation."

She wasn't certain she could do that, either, but simply acting like she would seemed to make her cousin happy enough.

"Don't get your hopes up, Erin. This has 'Lucy and Ethel' written all over it, and you know how their crazy schemes always turned out. I'm not going to jail for you, either. A Taylor with a criminal record would get even more press than one having to work a menial, nine-to-five job cleaning other people's bathrooms."

Two

This was insane.

She was a former socialite turned chambermaid, not some stealthy spy trained to ferret out classified information. She didn't even know what she was looking for, let alone how to find it.

Her cart was in the hall, but she'd dragged nearly everything she needed to clean and restock the room in with her. Sheets, towels, toilet paper, the vacuum cleaner… If there were enough supplies spread out, she figured she would look busier and have more of an excuse for moving all over the suite in case anyone—specifically Alexander Bajoran—came in and caught her poking around.

The problem was, his suite was pretty much immaculate. She'd been cleaning it herself on a daily basis, even before he'd checked in, and the Mountain View's housekeeping standards were quite high. Add to that the fact that Alexander

Bajoran was apparently quite tidy himself, and there was almost *nothing* personal left out for her to snoop through.

Regardless of what she'd let her cousin believe, she was not going to ransack this room. She would glance through the desk, under the bed, in the nightstands, maybe inside the closet, but she was not going to root through his underwear drawer. Not when she didn't even know what she was supposed to be looking for.

Business-related what? Compromising…what?

Jessica couldn't blame her cousin for wanting to find *something* incriminating. Anything that might turn the tables on the man who had destroyed the Taylors' livelihood and a few members of the family personally.

But how realistic was that, really? It had been five years since Bajoran's hostile takeover. He had moved on and was certainly juggling a dozen other deals and business ventures by now. And even if *those* weren't entirely on the level, she doubted he was walking around with a paper trail detailing his treachery.

The sheets were already pulled off the bed and in a heap on the floor, so it looked as though she was busy working. And since she was close, she quickly, quietly slid open one of the nightstand drawers.

Her hands were shaking, her fingertips ice-cold with nerves, and she was shivering in her plain white tennis shoes. Sure, she was alone, but the hallway door was propped open—as was lodge policy—and at any moment someone could walk in to catch her snooping.

She didn't know which would be worse—being caught by Alexander Bajoran or by her supervisor. One could kick up enough of a stink to get her fired…the other could fire her on the spot.

But she didn't need to worry too much right that second, because the drawer was empty. It didn't hold so much as a

Bible or telephone directory. Mountain View wasn't *that* kind of resort. If you needed a Bible or phone book or anything else—even items of a personal nature—you simply called the front desk and they delivered it immediately and with the utmost discretion.

Closing the drawer on a whisper, she kicked the soiled sheets out of her way and shook out the clean fitted sheet over the bare mattress as she rounded the foot of the bed. She covered one corner and then another before releasing the sheet to open the drawer of the opposite nightstand.

This one wasn't empty, and her heart stuttered in her chest at the knowledge that she was actually going to have to follow through on this. She was going to have to search through her family's archenemy's belongings.

The bottom drawer of the bedside bureau held a decanter of amber liquid—scotch, she presumed, though she'd never really been in charge of restocking the rooms' bars—and a set of highball glasses. The top drawer held a thick, leather-bound folder and dark blue Montblanc pen.

She swallowed hard. Once she moved that pen and opened the folder, that was it…she was invading Alexander's privacy and violating the employee agreement she'd signed when she'd first started working at the lodge.

Taking a deep breath, she closed her eyes for just a split second, then reached for the pen. As quickly as she could she flipped open the folder and tried to get her racing mind to make sense of the papers inside.

Her eyes skimmed the print of the first two pages, but nothing jumped out at her as being important or damaging. And the rest was just pictures of jewelry. Snapshots of finished pieces and sketches of what she assumed were proposed designs.

Beautiful, beautiful jewelry. The kind her family used to create. The kind she used to dream of being responsible for.

She'd grown up pampered and protected, and was pretty sure her parents had never expected her to do anything more than marry well and become the perfect trophy wife. But what she'd truly aspired to all those years she'd spent primping and attending finishing school was to actually work for Taylor Fine Jewels. Or possibly more specifically their partner company, Bajoran Designs.

Like any young woman, she loved jewelry. But where most of her peers had only wanted to wear the sparkly stuff, she'd wanted to *make* it. She loved sifting through cut and uncut gems to find the perfect stone for a setting she'd drawn herself.

All through high school her notebooks and the margins of her papers had been filled with intricate doodles that were in reality her ideas for jewelry designs. Her father had even used a few for pieces that had gone on to sell for six and seven figures. And for her sixteenth birthday, he'd surprised her with a pearl-and-diamond ring in a setting that had always been one of her very favorites.

It was still one of her favorites, though she didn't get many opportunities to wear it these days. Instead, it was tucked safely at the bottom of her jewelry box, hidden amongst the much less valuable baubles that suited her current level of income.

But, heavens above, these designs were beautiful. Not perfect. She could see where the size of one outshone the sapphire at its center. Or how the filigree of another was too dainty for the diamonds it surrounded.

She could fix the sketches with a sharp pencil and a few flicks of her wrist, and her palms itched to do just that.

When she caught herself running her fingers longingly across the glossy surface of one of the photographs, she sucked in a startled breath. How long had she been standing there with a target on her back? All she needed was for Alexander or another maid to walk in and catch her staring at his portfolio as if she was planning a heist.

Slamming the folder shut, she returned it to the bedside drawer and placed the pen back on top in exactly the same position it had been to begin with. She hoped.

With the nightstand put to rights, she finished stretching the fitted sheet over the other two corners of the mattress, then added the top sheet. She needed to get the room cleaned, and the best way to snoop was to search the areas nearest where she was working, anyway.

So she got the bedroom fixed up and cleaned but didn't resupply the bathroom before moving back into the main sitting room. She ran the vacuum over every inch of the rug, just like she was supposed to, but took her time and even poked the nose of the sweeper into the closet near the hallway door. The only thing she found there, however, was the hotel safe, which she knew she didn't stand a chance of getting into.

The only place left that might hold something of interest to her cousin was the large desk along the far wall. She'd avoided it until now because she suspected she didn't really want to find anything. She didn't want to be put in that spot between a rock and a hard place; didn't want to hand something over to Erin that might put her cousin in an even more precarious situation; didn't want to stir up trouble and poke at a sore spot within her family that *she'd* thought was beginning to heal over. She'd thought they were all moving on.

Apparently, she'd been wrong.

Leaving the vacuum nearby, she did a quick sweep of the top of the desk. There were a few sheets of hotel stationery with random notes written on them, but the rest seemed to be the typical items supplied by the lodge. Hotel directory, room-service menu, et cetera.

Inside the desk, though, she found a heck of a lot more.

Namely a small stack of manila folders and a laptop computer.

Jessica licked her lips, breathing in shallow bursts that matched the too-fast beat of her heart against her rib cage.

She was not opening that laptop, she just wasn't. For one thing, that would be *too much* breaking and entering, and sticking her nose where it didn't belong, for her peace of mind. For another, it would take too long. By the time it booted up and she figured out how to explore the different files and documents, her supervisor would surely be kicking in the door demanding to know why she was still in this suite when she should have been done with the entire floor.

She was sticking to her guns on this one. Erin might not like that decision, but she would just have to deal with it.

So she stuck with the folders lying beside the laptop, opening them one at a time and scanning them as quickly as possible.

Nothing jumped out at her as being out of the ordinary— not that she really had a clue what she was looking at or for. It was all just business jargon, and she certainly hadn't gone to business school.

But there was no mention of Taylor Fine Jewels in any of the papers…not that she'd expected there to be. And there was no indication of anything else that put her instincts on red alert.

She was just letting out a huff of air that was part frustration, part relief when she heard a creak and knew someone was entering the suite behind her. Her eyes flashed wide and she all but slammed the desk drawer shut—but slowly and quietly to keep from looking as guilty as she felt.

Putting her hand on the rag that she'd left on top of the desk, she started to wipe it down, just as she was supposed to. *Act natural. Act natural. Try not to hyperventilate. Act natural.*

Even though she knew darn well someone was behind her…likely standing there staring at her butt in the unappealing, lifeless gray smock that was her work uniform…she didn't react. She was alone, simply doing her job, as usual. The trick would be to feign surprise when she turned around and "discovered" that she *wasn't* alone.

Schooling her breathing…*act natural, act natural*…she hoped her cheeks weren't pink with the guilt of a kid caught with her hand in the cookie jar. Luck was on her side, though, because as she finished wiping down the desktop and twisted toward where she'd left the upright vacuum cleaner, whoever was standing behind her, silently monitoring her every move, cleared his throat.

And it was a he. She could tell by the timbre of that low rumble as it reached her ears and skated straight down her spine.

The air caught in her lungs for a moment, and she chastised herself for having such a gut-level, feminine response to something so simple. This man was a complete stranger. Her family's sworn enemy. And since he was a guest of Mountain View, and she worked for the lodge, he might as well be her employer.

Those were only the first of many reasons why her breathing should not be shallow, her blood should not be heating, and the clearing of his throat should not cause her to shiver inside her skin.

Doing her best to snap herself out of it, she straightened and twisted around, her hand still on the handle of the vacuum cleaner.

"Oh!" she exclaimed, letting her eyes go wide in mock startlement, praying the man standing in front of her wouldn't see right through it. "Hello again."

"Hello there," Alexander Bajoran returned, his mouth curving up in a small smile.

Jessica's pulse kicked up a notch.

It was nerves, she told herself. Just nerves.

But the truth was, the man was devilishly handsome. Enemy or no enemy, a blind woman would be able to see that.

His ink-black hair was perfectly styled, yet long enough in places to look relaxed and carefree. Eyes the color of blue ice glittered against skin that was surprisingly tan for a resident of the Pacific Northwest. But she knew for a fact it wasn't the result of time spent in tanning beds or spray-on booths; the entire Bajoran family leaned toward dark skin, dark hair... and ruthless personalities.

She had to remember that. The ruthless part, anyway.

Never mind how amazing he looked in his black dress slacks and dark blue blazer. Like he belonged on the cover of *GQ*. Or *Forbes,* thanks to his ill-gotten millions.

Never mind that if she saw him on the street, she would probably give herself whiplash spinning around to get a second look.

"We seem to have conflicting schedules this week," he said in a light, amused tone. His voice immediately touched deep, dark places inside of her that she *really* didn't want to think about.

He gave her a look, one she'd seen thousands of times in her adult life and had no trouble recognizing. Then his voice dropped a fraction, becoming sensual and suggestive.

"Or maybe they're matching up just right."

The heat of his voice was like sunshine on budding little seedlings, making *something* low in her belly shiver, quiver and begin to unfurl.

Oh, no. No, no, no. No more charming-but-dangerous men for her—and Alexander Bajoran was the most dangerous of all.

She'd been hit on and leered at by any number of male guests in her time at Mountain View. Traveling businessmen, vacationing husbands with a wandering eye, rich but useless playboys with a sense of entitlement…. But whether they'd pinched her on the rear, slipped her hundred-dollar tips or attempted simple flattery, she had never once been attracted to a single one of them.

Yet here she was, face-to-face with the man who had stolen her family's company and whom she was supposed to be spying on, and caterpillars were crawling around under every inch of her skin.

He took a step toward her, and her hands fisted, one around the handle of the vacuum, the other near her right hip. But all he did was set his briefcase—which was really more of a soft leather messenger bag—on the nearby coffee table before sinking into the overstuffed cushions of the sofa behind it.

Releasing a pent-up breath and sending some of those annoying creepy-crawlies away with it, Jessica reached down to unplug the sweeper and started to coil up the cord. The sooner she got out of there now that he was back, the better.

"I can leave you alone, if you need to work," she said, because the growing silence in the room was killing her.

But even though he had the brown leather satchel open on the glass-topped table and had pulled out several stacks of paperwork, he shook his head.

"Go ahead and finish what you were doing," he told her. "I've just got a couple of things to look over, but you won't distract me. In fact, the background noise might do me some good."

Well, shoot. How was she supposed to make a smooth but timely exit now?

She guessed she wasn't.

Dragging the vacuum across the sitting room, she set it in the hallway just outside the door of the suite. Then she gathered up an armful of fresh towels and washcloths for the bathroom.

It wasn't hard to go about her business this far away from Alexander. It was almost as though the air was normal in this tiled, insulated room instead of thick with nerves and guilt and unspoken sexual awareness. From her standpoint, at any rate. From his the air probably seemed absolutely normal. After all, he wasn't the one snooping, breaking the law, fighting a completely unwanted sexual attraction to someone he was supposed to hate.

She spent an inordinate amount of time making sure the towels hung just right on the towel rods and were perfectly even in their little cubbies under the vanity. Even longer putting out new bottles of shampoo, conditioner, mouthwash and shaving cream.

There were decorative mints and chocolates to go on the pillows in the bedroom, but she didn't want to go back in there. From the bathroom she could wave a hasty goodbye and get the heck out of Dodge. But if she returned to the bedroom, she would have to pass by Alexander. See him, smile at him, risk having him speak to her again.

That was one corner she was willing to cut today. Even if he complained to her superiors and she got in trouble later, missing mints were easier to apologize for than snooping or blushing herself into heat stroke in front of a valued guest.

Stepping out of the marble-and-gilt bathroom, she rounded the corner and was just congratulating herself on a narrow escape when she lifted her head and almost ran smack into Alexander, who was leaning against the outside wall waiting for her.

She made a tiny *eep* sound, slapping a hand over her heart as she bounced back on her heels.

"Sorry," he apologized, reaching out to steady her. "Didn't

mean to scare you, I just wanted to catch you before you took off."

If ever there was a word she didn't want to hear pass this man's lips, it was *catch*. Was she caught? Had he noticed something out of place? Figured out that she'd rifled through his things?

She held her breath, waiting for the accusations he had every right to fling at her.

Instead, as soon as he was sure she wasn't going to topple over, he let go of her elbow and went back to leaning negligently against the wall. It was a casual pose, but all Jessica could think was that he was standing between her and the door, blocking her only exit from the suite.

"I know this is probably out of line," he murmured, "but I was hoping you'd have dinner with me tonight."

His words caused her heart to stutter and then stall out completely for several long seconds.

"I'm here on business, so after I finish with meetings and such during the day, my evening hours are a bit…empty."

He shrugged a shoulder, and because he'd taken off the blazer, she could see the play of muscle caused by the movement beneath his crisp white dress shirt. Something so minor shouldn't make her hormones sit up and take notice, but they did. Boy, howdy, did they ever.

Licking her lips, she cleared her throat and hoped her voice didn't squeak when she tried to speak. It was bad enough that her face was aflame with nerves; she could feel the heat all but setting her eyelashes on fire. She already looked like a clown, in many people's estimation—she didn't need to open her mouth and sound like one, too.

"Thank you, but fraternizing with guests is against resort policy."

Ooh, that sounded good. Very confident and professional—and squeak-free.

Alexander lifted a brow. "Somehow I find it hard to believe a woman with blue hair is afraid of breaking a few rules."

She reached up to toy with the strip of chemically altered hair he was referring to. "It's not *all* blue," she muttered.

That bought her a too-handsome grin and flash of very white, perfectly straight teeth. "Just enough to let the world know you're a rebel, right?"

Wow, he had her pegged, didn't he? And he wasn't taking no, thank you, for an answer.

Dropping the hank of hair, Jessica pushed her shoulders back. She was a rebel, as well as a confident, self-reliant woman. But she wasn't stupid.

"I could lose my job," she said simply.

He cocked his head. She wasn't the only self-assured person in the room.

"But you won't," he told her matter-of-factly. Then, after a brief pause, he added, "Would it make you feel better if I said I won't let that happen?"

With anybody else she would have scoffed. But knowing who Alexander Bajoran was and the power he held—even here in Portland—she had no doubt he meant what he said and had enough influence to make it stick.

"You'll be on your own time, not the resort's," he pointed out. "And I'll let you decide whether we order from room service or go out somewhere else."

She should say no. Any sensible person would. The entire situation screamed danger with a capital *D*.

But she had to admit, she was curious. She'd had male guests proposition her before, give her that salacious, skin-crawling look reserved for when they were on out-of-town business trips without their wives and thought they could get away with something.

Alexander was the first, though, to ask her to dinner without the creepy looks or attempts at groping. Which made her wonder why he was interested.

Did he suspect her of snooping around where she didn't belong, or was he just hitting on a pretty, no-strings-attached maid? Did he recognize her as a Taylor and think she was up to something, or just hope to get lucky?

Of course she *was* up to something, but now she wanted to know if *he* was up to something, too.

So even though she knew she should be running a hundred miles an hour in the opposite direction, she opened her mouth and made the biggest mistake of her life.

"All right."

Three

Jessica didn't get many opportunities to dress up these days. But she was having dinner this evening with a very wealthy, very handsome man, and even though she knew it was a terrible idea, she wanted to make the most of it. Not so much the man and the dinner but simply the act of going out and feeling special for a little while. Putting on something pretty rather than functional. Taking extra time with her makeup and hair. Wearing heels instead of ratty old tennies.

She even went so far as to dab on a couple drops of what was left of her favorite three-hundred-dollar-an-ounce designer perfume, Fanta C. Alexander Bajoran might not be worth a spritz or two, but she certainly was.

She was wearing a plain black skirt and flowy white blouse with a long, multi-strand necklace and large gold hoop earrings in her primary holes. The others held her usual array of studs and smaller hoops.

As she strode down the carpeted hallway, she fiddled with

every part of her outfit. Was her skirt too short? Did her blouse show too much cleavage? Would the necklace draw Alexander's eye to her breasts? Or worse yet, would the earrings pull too much of his attention to her face?

Flirting—even flirting with danger this way—was one thing. Truly risking being recognized by her family's greatest enemy, though… No, she didn't want that.

Which was why she'd chosen to meet him here, in his room at the resort, rather than going out to a public restaurant where they might be seen by someone they—especially she—knew.

Getting caught in a guest's room after work hours would be bad, but being spotted out on a date with Alexander by one of her relatives or somebody who might tell one of her relatives would be exponentially worse. She would rather be fired than deal with the familial fallout.

Reaching the door of his suite, Jessica stopped and took a deep breath. She straightened her clothes and jewelry for the thousandth time and checked her small clutch purse to be sure she had her cell phone, a lipstick, a few bucks just in case. She didn't know if she would end up needing any of those things, but wanted to have them, all the same.

When there was nothing left to double-check, no other reason to put off the inevitable, she took another deep, stabilizing breath, held it and let it out slowly as she tapped on the door.

The nerves she'd tamped down started to wiggle back toward the surface as she waited for him to answer. Then suddenly the door swung open, and there he was.

Six foot something of dark, imposing good-looks. Slacks still smooth and pressed, despite being worn all day. Pale, pale lavender dress shirt unbuttoned at his throat and sleeves rolled up to his elbows, but no less distinguished than when he'd been wearing a tie and suit jacket.

He smiled in welcome and a lump formed in her throat, making it hard to swallow. Suddenly she was almost pathologically afraid to be alone with him. It was two mature adults sharing a simple meal, but almost as though she was watching a horror movie, she could see around all the corners to where scary things and maniacal killers waited.

A thousand frightening scenarios and terrible outcomes flitted through her brain in the nanosecond it took him to say hello—or rather, a deep, masculine, "Hi, there"—and step back to let her into the suite.

She could have run. She could have begged off, hurriedly telling him she'd changed her mind, or that something important had come up and she couldn't stay.

She probably should have.

Instead, a tiny voice in her head whispered, *What's the worst that can happen?* and showed her images of a lovely, delicious meal at an establishment where she worked but never got the chance to indulge, with an attractive man the likes of which she probably wouldn't meet again for a very long time. Not given her current circumstances.

So she didn't run. She told herself she was here, he was a gentleman, and everything would be fine.

"Thank you," she murmured, surprised when her voice not only didn't crack, but came out in a low, almost smoky tone that sounded a lot sexier than she'd intended.

She stepped into the suite, and he closed the door behind her with a soft click. More familiar with these rooms than she cared to admit, she moved down the short hallway and into the sitting room where there was already a table set up with white linens and covered silver serving trays.

"I hope you don't mind, but I took the liberty of ordering," Alexander said, coming up behind her. "I thought it would save some time."

True enough. Mountain View employed one of the best

chefs in the country and served some of the best food on the West Coast, but room service was room service. It sometimes took longer than guests might have liked for their meals to arrive, especially if the kitchen was busy trying to get food out to the dining room.

Cupping her elbow, he steered her around the table and pulled out her chair. She tried not to let the heat of his hand do funny things to her pulse. Of course, her pulse had a mind of its own.

He helped her get seated, then began uncovering plates of food. The smells hit her first, and they were divine. Even before she could identify them all, she saw that he'd ordered a sampling of some of the very best culinary creations the resort had to offer.

From the appetizer section of the menu he'd asked for watermelon gazpacho with tomato; cucumber and borage; seafood tomato bisque; eggplant ravioli; and oysters in red wine mignonette.

As entrées, he'd gone with pheasant with green cabbage, port wine-infused pear and black truffle shavings, and something she could rarely resist—crab cakes. Mountain View's particular recipe consisted of large chunks of Dungeness crab, tiny bits of lobster, corn and faro lightly seared to a golden brown.

He had no way of knowing they were one of her all-time favorites, though. Most likely he'd ordered them because they were nearly world renowned and one of the most popular items on the resort's menu.

But her stomach rumbled and her mouth began to water at the very sight. She might work here, might have skated past the kitchen or dining room a time or two, but since she couldn't exactly afford fifty-dollar-a-plate dinners any longer, she'd never been lucky enough to actually taste them.

"I hope there's something here you'll like."

Like? She wanted to take her clothes off and roll around on the table of food, then lick her body clean.

Because she wasn't certain she could speak past the drool pooling on her tongue, she merely nodded and made an approving *mmm-hmm* sound.

"I ordered dessert, as well, but let's wait until we finish this before we dig into that."

Oh. She'd heard wonderful things about Mountain View's desserts, too.

"So…" he murmured, "where would you like to start? Or should I just hand over the crab cakes before someone gets hurt?"

The mention of crab cakes and the slight amusement in his tone brought her head up, and she realized she'd been concentrating rather intensely on that particular platter.

"Sorry, they just…smell really good."

He grinned at her candid response. Reaching to the side and lifting the plate, he set it back down directly in front of her.

"They're all yours," he told her. "As long as you don't mind if I keep the pheasant to myself."

Well, she would have liked at least a *tiny* bite—she'd never had the pleasure of trying that particular dish, either—but if the crab cakes were as delicious as they looked, smelled and she'd heard they were, she supposed it was a sacrifice worth making.

Her silence seemed to be answer enough. He moved the pheasant to his place setting, then reached for the bottle of wine in the center of the table and pulled the cork. While she shook out her napkin and laid it across her lap, he poured two glasses of the rich, dark liquid and handed one to her.

She took it with a murmured thank-you and brought it to her nose for a sniff. Mmm. It had been a while since she'd enjoyed a glass of really good, expensive wine. This one was full-bodied, with the scents of fruit, spice and just a hint of chocolate.

She was tempted to take a sip right away, but didn't want to ruin her first taste of the crab cakes and had also promised herself she would be careful tonight. A little bit of wine with dinner wouldn't hurt, but she didn't want to risk drinking too much and forgetting who she was...who he was... and exactly how much was on the line if she accidentally let any part of the truth slip past her lips.

So she set the glass aside and picked up her fork instead.

"At the risk of scaring you off now that you're already here," Alexander said, shaking out his own napkin and placing it across his lap, "it occurred to me that I invited you to dinner tonight without even knowing your name. Or introducing myself, for that matter."

Jessica paused with her first bite of crab cake halfway to her mouth. Uh-oh. She hadn't been concerned with introducing herself to Alexander because she already knew who he was. And keeping her own identity under wraps was critical, so she hadn't exactly been eager to share that information, either.

Now, however, she was cornered, and she'd better come up with a response soon or he would start to get suspicious.

To buy herself a little bit of time, she continued the trajectory of her fork and went ahead with that first bite of food she'd so been looking forward to. Her anticipation was dampened slightly by the tension thrumming through her body and causing her mind to race, but that didn't keep her taste buds from leaping with joy at the exquisite spices and textures filling her mouth.

Oh, this was so worth the stress and subterfuge of pretending to be someone she wasn't. With luck she would only have to lie to him for one night, and not only would he be none the wiser, but she'd have the experience of a lovely meal with a handsome, wealthy playboy-type tucked away in her memory banks.

The part about deceiving him and searching his suite like a wannabe spy would maybe have to be deleted, if she hoped to live with herself for the next fifty years, though.

Making a satisfied sound deep in her throat, she swallowed and finally turned her attention to Alexander—since she couldn't justify ignoring him any longer.

"My name is Jessica. Madison," she told him, using her middle name instead of her last. If he questioned anyone at the resort, they would either deny knowing her or correct her little fib without realizing they were revealing anything significant. He obviously hadn't asked around about her or he would already know her name, and she doubted he would bother after this, as long as she didn't give him cause to become curious.

He offered her a small grin and held his hand out across the table. She had to put her fork down to take it.

"Hello, Jessica. I'm Alexander Bajoran. You can call me Alex."

A shiver of heat went through her at both the familiarity of his invitation and the touch of his smooth, warm hand.

Darn it! Why did she have to like him so much? And she really did. He was charming and good-looking and self-assured. Knowing he had a nice, hefty bank account certainly didn't hurt, but it was his easy friendliness that made her regret her bargain with Erin and the fact that she was a Taylor.

If she didn't have that baggage, she suspected she would be extremely flattered by his apparent interest in her and excited about tonight's "date." But she would be self-conscious about the fact that she was a lowly chambermaid, while he was clearly blessed financially, even though there was a time when her fiscal worth possibly rivaled his own.

She would have been fidgeting in her seat, careful to say

and do all the right things in hopes of having him ask her out again.

And she probably also would have been imagining going to bed with him. Maybe not tonight, on their first date, or even on their second or third. But eventually—and sooner rather than later considering her deep and sudden hormonal reaction to him.

Shifting in her chair, she returned her attention to her plate, playing with her food in an attempt to get her rioting emotions under control. Not for the first time, she realized how truly foolish it was for her to have agreed to spend any more time alone with him than absolutely necessary.

Alexander—Alex—didn't seem to be suffering from any such second guesses, however.

"So…" he muttered casually, digging into his own perfectly roasted pheasant. "Tell me something about yourself. Were you born here in Portland? Did you grow up here? What about your family?"

All loaded questions, littered with pitfalls that could land her in very hot water. Without getting too detailed or giving away anything personal, she told him what she could, stretching the truth in some places and avoiding it altogether in others.

Before long, their plates were clean, their glasses of wine had been emptied and refilled at least once and they were chatting comfortably. More comfortably than Jessica ever would have expected. Almost like new friends. Or new ones, hoping to become even more….

Four

Reaching across the table, Alex topped off Jessica's glass before emptying the rest of the bottle into his own. He leaned back in his chair, watching her, letting the bouquet of the expensive wine fill his nostrils while his eyes took in every detail of the woman sitting before him.

He couldn't remember a time when he'd enjoyed a dinner more. So many of his meals were spent with business acquaintances, hammering out a new deal, discussing the aspects of a new publicity campaign or simply blowing smoke up someone's proverbial skirt in an effort to preserve continued goodwill. Even dinner with his family tended toward business talk over anything personal.

Jessica, however, was a breath of much-needed fresh air. Without a doubt she was a beautiful woman. It was hard to miss her streak of blue hair or the multiple piercings running along her ear lobes and right eyebrow, but rather than detracting from her attractiveness, they added a unique flare to her classic good looks.

She was also much smarter and more well-spoken than he would have expected from a hotel maid. Truth be told, he hadn't known what to expect from the evening after his completely impromptu invitation. But Jessica was turning out to be quite entertaining. Not only were her anecdotes amusing, but her warm, whiskey-soft voice was one he wouldn't mind hearing more of. For how long, he wasn't sure. The rest of the night might be nice. Possibly even in the morning over breakfast.

Jessica chuckled at whatever she'd just said—something he'd missed because he was preoccupied by the glossy pink of her bow-shaped mouth, the smooth half-moons of her neat but unmanicured nails and the soft bounce of her honey-blond curls. She tucked one of the shoulder-length strands behind her ear and licked those delectable lips, and Alex nearly shot straight up out of his chair. And while he managed—barely—to remain seated, other portions of his anatomy were beginning to inch their way north.

Knowing his behavior probably came across as bordering on strange, he shot to his feet, nearly tipping the heavy armchair over in the process. In the next instant he'd grabbed her hand and yanked her up, as well.

She made a small sound of surprised protest, but didn't resist. She did, however, dig in her heels and catch herself on the edge of the table just before she would have smacked straight into his chest.

Too bad; he would have liked to feel her pressed against him for a moment or two. Her warmth, her curves, the swell of her breasts.

When he'd walked into his suite to find her making his bed that first time, he'd caught a whiff of lemon and thought it came from whatever cleaning solutions she'd been using.

Now he realized the tangy scent had nothing to do with dusting or scrubbing. Instead, it came directly from her. From her shampoo or perfume, or maybe both. It was a peculiar blend of citrus and flowers that he'd never smelled before, but that seemed to suit her perfectly.

He took a deep breath to bring even more of the intoxicating fragrance into his lungs, then reached around her to pick up both glasses of wine.

"Come on," he invited, tipping his head toward the French doors and the balcony beyond.

He left her to follow—or not—but was pleased when she did. Even more pleased that it seemed to take her no time at all to decide. No sooner had he turned and started walking than she was on his heels.

Though Jessica had arrived while it was still light out, the sun had long ago slipped beyond the horizon, leaving the sky dark and star dappled. A slight breeze chilled the evening air, but nothing that required jackets or would hinder them from enjoying being outside for a while.

Moving to the stone balustrade, he set down the two glasses, then turned, leaning back on his rear and crossing his arms over his chest. As large as the Mountain View resort was, and as many guests as he was sure were in residence, the wide balcony that ran the entire length of his suite was completely private.

Tall, waffle-patterned trellises protected either side from the balconies beyond. He didn't know what the lodge did about them in the dead of winter, but at this time of year, they were covered with climbing flowering vines, creating a natural barrier to sound and sight.

When Jessica came close enough that he could have reached out and touched her, he uncrossed his arms and reached behind him instead. "Your wine," he offered in a low voice.

She took it, raising it to her mouth to sip. For long minutes neither of them said anything. Then she moved to the low chaise longue a few feet away and carefully lowered herself to its cushioned seat.

Her skirt rode up, flashing an extra couple of inches of smooth thigh. More than he'd been able to see while she'd cleaned his rooms in that frumpy gray uniform. A shame, too, since she had *amazing* legs. Long and sleek and deliciously toned.

He had the sudden urge to sit down next to her and run his hand along that silken length. Even through her stockings he wanted to feel the curve of her knee, the sensitive dip beneath, the line of her outer thigh and the perilous trail inside.

Alex sucked in a breath, his mouth gone suddenly dry.

When was the last time he'd been this attracted to a woman? Any woman?

He'd had affairs, certainly. A few relationships, even. At one time, he'd dated a woman long enough to consider marrying her. He hadn't loved her, not really, but it had seemed as if it might be the right thing to do. The most sensible next step, at any rate.

He was no stranger to lust, either. He'd been with women who'd caused it to flare hot and fast. But to the best of his recollection, he'd never been with a woman who stimulated his libido *and* his brain both at the same time.

Oh, it wasn't as though he and Jessica were waxing poetic about astrophysics or the effect of global warming on penguins in Antarctica. But that was just the point: he'd *had* those discussions—or similar ones, at least—with certain women without a single erotic nerve ending tingling to life. Just as he'd found himself burning with passion and rolling around on the sheets with others without a single intelligent thought passing between them.

And then there was Jessica Madison. Nearly anonymous

housekeeper at a resort he'd only decided to patronize a week and a half ago. If he'd booked a suite at the downtown Hilton instead, as had been his first inclination, he never would have bumped into her.

Damned if he wasn't glad they'd been booked up and someone had recommended Mountain View as a second choice. This dinner alone was worth every penny of the added expense and every extra mile it took to get into downtown Portland for his scheduled meetings.

Jessica wasn't just lovely to look at, but entertaining, too. Not only conversationally but in her silent self-assurance.

The hair and jewelry choices were the physical aspects of that, he supposed; a way to tell the world without words that she knew who she was and didn't care what anyone thought of her or how she lived her life. But whether she realized it or not, her body language conveyed the same message.

Once she'd spotted those crab cakes and decided she wanted them, it had been difficult to draw her attention away from the plate. And when he'd told her she could have them all to herself, she'd set about eating them as passionately as an artist struck by sudden creative inspiration.

No worries about how she'd looked or what he might think. Which wasn't to say she'd been a ravenous wolf about it. Her table manners had been flawless. But she'd enjoyed her meal the way he enjoyed a quick bout of neat, no-strings lovemaking.

And there it was. Sex. No matter where his mind started to wander when he got to thinking about this woman, it always seemed to circle right back around to *S-E-X*.

It didn't help that she was stretching now, lifting her legs onto the long seat of the chaise and leaning back until she was nearly sprawled out like a virgin sacrifice.

Blood pooled in his groin, heating, thrumming, creating a beat in his veins that matched the one in his brain. *Pa-dump.*

Pa-dump. Pa-dump. His heart, his pulse and his head kept the same rhythm, one that he could have sworn was saying, *Do it, do it, do it.*

He was very afraid "it" could be defined as something ill-advised. Like kissing her. Touching her. Taking her to bed.

Indulging in another sip of wine, Jessica let out a breathy sigh and crossed her legs—those damn tempting legs—at the ankle. She rested her arms on the armrests and her head back against the chaise.

"I'm sorry," she said. "I've been doing all the talking and not letting you get a word in edgewise."

Something he'd noticed, but certainly hadn't minded. He'd much rather listen to her speak than himself. On his best day he was a man of few words, and his only response now was to arch his brow and lift his own wine to his mouth for a drink.

"So…" she prompted. "Tell me about yourself. What do you do? Why are you in town? How long will you be staying at our fine establishment?"

"How long will you be making my bed and restocking my wet bar, you mean?" he retorted with a grin.

She chuckled, the sound filling the night air and doing nothing to quiet the pounding in his blood, his head, his gut.

"I don't stock the bars," she told him, returning his grin. "They don't trust us near the pricey liquor—because they're afraid we'll either steal it…or drink on the job."

He laughed at that. "I might be tempted to drink, too, if I had to clean up after strangers all day. Especially the kind who stay here. I imagine a lot of us come across as quite demanding and entitled."

She shrugged a shoulder. "It's not so bad. For one thing, I don't usually have to interact with you demanding, entitled types. Most of the time the rooms are empty when I clean, and I get to work alone. The pay could be better—and for rich people, you guys sure can cheap out when it comes to tipping—but I like my coworkers, and the view is stunning when I get the chance to stop and actually enjoy it."

He inclined his head. "Duly noted. In the future, I'll be sure to leave a generous tip anytime I stay out of town."

"Every morning before you leave your room," she clarified, "not just the day you check out. Shifts change, and the same maids don't always clean the same rooms every day."

As hard as he tried, he couldn't completely hold back the hint of a smile. She was a pretty good advocate for her fellow service workers.

"I'll remember that. Have my tips so far been acceptable?" he asked, half teasing, half genuinely curious of her opinion.

She slanted her head, thinking about it for a minute. Then she shrugged a shoulder. "You've been doing well enough. And tonight's dinner definitely makes up for any corners you may have cut."

"Glad to hear it," he drawled.

"You never answered my question," she said after a moment of silence passed. The only sounds in the growing darkness were the muted voices of guests far off in the distance, perhaps strolling along one of the lodge's moonlit paths, and the occasional chirp of crickets.

"Which one?"

"Any of them. All of them." She uncrossed her ankles only to cross them again the other way. "Just tell me something interesting so I won't feel like I monopolized the conversation tonight."

"All right," he replied. Pushing away from the stone barrier, he strode toward her, dragging the second chaise closer to hers one-handed and sitting down on the very end to face her.

"My family is in jewelry. Gems and design. Maybe you've heard of us—Bajoran Designs?"

Her eyes widened. "*You're* Bajoran Designs?"

"I'm one of the Bajorans of Bajoran Designs," he clarified. "As much as I might feel or wish otherwise at times, it isn't a one-man operation."

"Wow. Your jewelry is amazing."

"You're familiar with it?"

"Isn't everybody?" she retorted. "Your ads are in all the magazines, and on TV and billboards everywhere. Didn't you design a bracelet for the Queen of England or something?"

"Again, *I* didn't, but our company did."

"Wow," she repeated. And then her head tilted to one side and she raised a brow. Her lips curved. "I don't suppose you have any free samples you'd like to share."

The sparkle in her eyes told him she was teasing, but he wished suddenly that he had more than just a few proposed design sketches with him. He wished he had a briefcase full of priceless jewels surrounded by exquisite settings to regale her with.

He would love to see her draped in emeralds and platinum or diamonds and gold. Earrings, necklace, bracelet, perhaps even a small tiara to tuck into those mostly blond curls.

He could think of any number of his companies' designs that would look stunning with what she was wearing. But he imagined that they'd look even better on her while she was utterly naked.

Naked in his bed, her skin alabaster against dark sheets, her hair falling loosely about her shoulders. And at her lobes, her throat, her waist…maybe her ankle, too…*his* jewels, *his* designs, in essence his *marks* lying cool on her warm, flushed flesh.

The picture that filled his head was vibrant and erotic and so real, he nearly reached out to touch her, fully expecting to encounter nothing but the blessed nudity of a gorgeous and waiting female.

Arousal smacked into him with the force of a freight train

late to its final destination. His fist closed on the wine in his hand, so tight he was surprised the glass didn't shatter. Every muscle in his body turned to iron, and that most important one—the one that desired her most of all—came to attention in a way that made its wishes clearly known.

Sweat broke out across Alex's brow and his lungs hitched with the effort to breathe. Jessica was still staring at him, the amusement at her teasing about the jewelry slowly seeping from her eyes as she realized he wasn't laughing.

She probably thought she'd insulted him. Or come across as a gold digger. The difference in their stations—her minimum wage chambermaid to his multimillionaire business tycoon—was patently obvious, and something he supposed she hadn't forgotten for a minute. Add to that the fact that he felt ready to explode, and he probably looked like Dr. Jekyll well on his way to becoming Mr. Hyde.

Forcing himself to loosen his grip on the wineglass, he concentrated on his breathing. *Relax,* he told himself. *Breathe in, breathe out. Don't scare her off before you have a chance to seduce her.*

And he was going to seduce her. He'd been attracted to her from the moment they'd first met, which, of course, meant he'd thought about sleeping with her about a thousand times since. But thinking about it and making a conscious decision to go through with it were two different things.

He hadn't realized until just this minute that he *was* going to make a move on her. He *was* going to kiss her and do his best to convince her to go to bed with him.

Pushing to his feet, he leaned across to set his wine on the wrought-iron table that had been between the two chaises. He locked his jaw and cursed himself when she jerked at his sudden movements. His only hope was that he hadn't frightened her so much that he couldn't smooth things over. Seducing a woman on the first date could be hard enough without adding "acted like a jackass" to the mix.

"Sorry," he said in a low voice, hoping the single word would be suitable as a blanket apology. And then in answer to her earlier question, "I don't have any samples. I'd need a 24/7 armed guard to carry that kind of merchandise around with me."

At his friendly tone, she seemed to relax. And when she did, he did.

"If you like, though, I can arrange a tour of our company. You can see how the pieces are put together, watch some gems being cut, maybe even catch a peek at a few designs that haven't been released yet. You'd have to come to Seattle, though. Think you can get the time off?"

If he'd expected her to be impressed, he was sorely disappointed. Her expression barely changed as her tongue darted out to lick her lips.

"That's all right," she said, instead of "Oh, wow, that would be awesome!" "I was just joking. I could never afford anything of yours, anyway. Better not to tempt myself."

It was on the tip of his tongue to tell her he'd gift her with a piece while she was there. He'd never done anything of the sort before, never even been tempted. Yet suddenly he didn't want to just imagine her covered in his family's fine jewelry, he wanted to literally cover her with it. Throw it at her feet like a humble servant making an offering to the gods. Diamonds, emeralds, opals, sapphires… Whatever she wanted. As much as she wanted.

He wasn't sure exactly when he'd become such a weak-kneed sycophant. He'd certainly never given women jewelry before; at least not easily or as willy-nilly as he was envisioning doing with Jessica.

To be honest, he wasn't sure he liked these feelings and the lack of control she seemed to evoke. It was the number one reason he thought he should probably call it a night and get as far away as possible from this woman.

That would be the smart thing to do, for certain.

So why didn't he?

Desire? Lust? Sheer stupidity?

But rather than thank her for coming and seeing her to the door, he held out his hand, indicating that she should give him her wineglass. When she did, he set it aside, then held out his hand again, this time inviting her to take it. He was equal parts surprised and relieved when she did so without a hint of reservation that he could detect.

Her fingers were cool and delicate. For a moment he savored the simple touch, not letting himself ruin it by imagining more just yet.

Then he gave her a tug, urging her to the edge of the chaise. A second tug pulled her to her feet.

She came into his arms as though she was tied to him and he was drawing on the string that bound them. Another step and she was pressed to his chest the way he'd wished she could be earlier.

Her blouse was silky against his palms and the front of his own dress shirt, her breasts rubbing just enough to give him ideas and get the blood pumping hot and thick to his groin once again. He held her there, enjoying the feel of her, stroking his hands up and down the line of her spine.

To his great delight she didn't pull away, but sank into him even more, her breath blowing out on a soft sigh.

With one hand at the small of her back, he brought the other up the length of her arm and the side of her throat until he cupped her jaw, his thumb brushing along the baby-soft curve of her cheek.

"I want to kiss you," he told her in a low, graveled voice, "but I'm afraid you'll think I'm moving too fast."

Afraid he was moving too fast and that he would scare her

off. Afraid that this overwhelming need he felt for her wasn't normal, wasn't the typical interest he felt when he was in the mood for a one-night stand.

"Did you notice my hair?" Jessica asked in little more than a murmur, reaching up to finger a few strands of blue.

His brows knit. What did her hair have to do with anything?

Still, he answered, "Yes."

"And my ears? My brow?" She flicked her wrist at both.

"Yes," he said again, more confused than ever.

"These are not the piercings and hairstyle choices of a girl who scares easily."

For a second, he didn't move, didn't dare breathe while her words sank in. Then a slow smile spread across his face.

"No," he murmured, even as his head lowered toward hers. "I guess they aren't."

Five

The minute Alex's lips touched hers, she was lost.

She knew this was a mistake. Everything was, from the moment she'd stepped into his suite tonight, to letting her guard down over wine and a moonlit stroll onto the secluded balcony. Maybe even before that, when she'd recognized him and not gone running, or when she'd agreed to her cousin's ridiculous scheme.

It hadn't been easy to sit still and pretend she didn't know who he was, but it *had* been somewhat enlightening to listen to him talk about himself and his business. Knowing what she did about him—namely that he'd stolen a portion of the company out from under her family—she would have expected him to be proud, arrogant, boastful.

Instead, he'd been humble, speaking highly of Bajoran Designs, but not taking any of the credit for the company's success for himself.

She thought that might have been when her head had

started to go fuzzy and stars had formed in her eyes. Her skin had been flushed with heat, too, but that was nothing new; that was just part of the attraction that had flared to life as soon as she'd walked into his arms.

She shouldn't be kissing him…or rather, allowing him to kiss her. It was a worse idea than agreeing to dinner with him, but she just couldn't seem to help herself.

The entire time they'd been talking, all she'd wanted was to cross the balcony and lay a hand on his chest. To see if it felt as hot and hard as it looked. And then to touch his mouth with her own to see if he tasted as delectable as she imagined.

The good news was, his chest *did* feel as hot and hard as she'd thought it would. Better, even, pressed up against her breasts and her belly.

And his lips were as delicious as she'd expected. Warm and soft but with a firmness that spoke of power and total self-confidence. He also tasted of the lush wine and food they'd shared earlier.

The *bad* news was that his chest felt exactly as she'd imagined, his mouth tasted even better, and instead of allaying her curiosity, it only made her want more.

With a groan she leaned farther into him, letting his heat and strong arms surround her, letting the passion sweep her away.

It was just a kiss, just one night, and he had no idea who she really was. What could it hurt to surrender to whatever this was igniting between them and just let go?

She didn't let her mind wander past that, didn't let her brain actually consider all the things that really could go wrong. She didn't want to think about it, didn't want to slow down—or worse, stop. For once she wanted to let go, be wild, be free and not worry about the consequences.

Besides, it wasn't as though anyone would ever find out. Erin would think she'd searched Alex's suite and come up with nothing, and Alex would think he'd gotten lucky with a near-anonymous hotel maid. No strings, no ties, no awkward morning after.

His mouth possessed her, but she certainly didn't mind. If anything, her moan, the melt of her body, her meeting his tongue swipe for swipe and thrust for thrust told him exactly how much she liked it.

Liked it? Loved it and was eager for more.

Not bothering to breathe—who needed oxygen?—Jessica wrapped her arms around Alex's neck, running her fingers through the hair at his nape and hanging on for dear life.

It was Alex's turn to groan. He hugged her tight and she felt his arousal standing proud, leaving no doubt that he was just as turned on as she was, just as carried away on this wave of uncontrollable lust.

Thank goodness. She would hate to be coiled in a haze of desire, only to discover he'd been after nothing more than a quick kiss.

But she needn't have worried. He was all but sucking her tonsils down his throat. And then his hands went to her waist, her hips, her thighs a second before he scooped her into his arms.

They broke apart, only because the change of position forced it, and it turned out people really did need oxygen eventually. They both gasped for breath as he carried her across the balcony and through the French doors, his long strides eating up the thickly carpeted floor all the way to the bedroom.

Once there, he set her on the end of the wide, king-size bed with more gentleness than she would have managed if their roles had been reversed. Standing over her, he stared into her eyes, his own crystal-blue ones blazing like hot ice.

With both hands, he cupped her face, tipping her head

back a fraction of an inch. Then he leaned in and kissed her softly, almost reverently.

Jessica's eyes slid closed, letting the sensation of his lips on hers wash over her, carrying her away.

A moment later, his mouth left her, but she felt his hands at her throat, his fingers trailing down the sides, over her collarbones and the slope of her chest. Goose bumps broke out on her skin as he grazed the insides of her breasts and started to unbutton her blouse.

She held her breath while he worked. This wasn't the first time a man had undressed her, but it was certainly the first time one had done it so slowly and had seemed to take such pleasure in the act. Either that or he was torturing her, but even the torture brought exquisite pleasure.

When he reached the last of the buttons, she straightened enough for him to tug the blouse from the waistband of her skirt. He flicked it over her shoulders and arms, then tossed it away completely.

Sitting there in her skirt and bra, Jessica suddenly realized she didn't have to be so passive. As much as she was enjoying his seductive treatment, she wanted to be in on the action. And, yes—if she was soon going to be naked in front of him, then she wanted to see him out of his clothes, too.

While he went for the zipper at the back of her skirt, she went for his belt buckle. He sucked air through his teeth, and she was delighted to see his nostrils flare, his jaw tic.

After undoing his belt, she got to work on his fly. She slid the tab down so slowly, each individual snick of the zipper's teeth echoed through the room. He was just as deliberate unzipping her skirt.

He pulled her to her feet by the elbows, tugging her against his chest again while he slipped the skirt past her hips. At the same time, he kicked off his shoes, letting her push his pants down so that both items of clothing fell to the floor together.

He set her back on the bed, then stepped out of the pants and kicked their clothes out of the way, unbuttoning his shirt and shrugging out of it all with urgent efficiency. Standing before her totally naked, Alex stared down at her with fire in his eyes and a set to his tall frame that told her without words that there was no turning back now. No escape.

As though she'd even want to. If she hadn't been sitting already, Jessica was pretty sure she would have melted into a steaming puddle on the floor. Her knees were jelly, her stomach doing somersaults worthy of an Olympic gold medal.

Her mouth felt as if it was filled with sand, and she licked her lips, swallowing in an attempt to bring some moisture back before the dehydration went to her head and sent her into a dead faint.

His gaze zeroed in on that tiny gesture, and she could have sworn she saw smoke spiraling out of his ears. He took a single, purposeful step toward her, bringing himself flush with the foot of the bed. Leaning in, he towered over her, fists flat on the mattress on either side of her hips.

"Scoot up," he told her in a low voice.

Even though her bones felt like rubber, she put her hands under her and did as he'd ordered, slowing moving back across the mattress toward the head of the bed. He followed her every inch of the way. Hovering over her, crawling with her, plucking the heels off her feet and pitching them over his shoulder as they went. She stopped when she reached the pillows, letting her head sink into one of the feather-stuffed cushions, still covered by the spread she'd tucked around them that morning.

"You're overdressed," Alex murmured a moment before he tucked his thumbs into the waistband of her barely there satin-and-lace panties and drew them down her legs. She helped him by kicking them off, then lifted up so he could unclasp and remove her bra.

For several long seconds he drank her in, his gaze so intense, she could hardly breathe. Just when she was about to hide her breasts self-consciously with her arms, Alex reached around her, loosening the bed's comforter and dragging it down, uncovering the pillows and sliding the slick fabric under her body until they were resting only on cool, freshly laundered sheets.

Once he was happy with the state of the bed, he lowered himself down on top of her. From chest to ankle he covered her like a blanket, the heat of his skin warming her and the hairs on his legs and chest tickling in all the right places.

He offered her a small, confident smile, and she couldn't resist rubbing against him, loving every single seductive sensation. Then she looped her arms around his shoulders and met him for a long, deep, soul-rattling kiss.

Alex ate at her mouth like he was enjoying their succulent dinner all over again. And she licked back as though she had moved on to the most decadent of desserts.

Alex's hands skimmed her body, up and down, all around, learning her shape and form and sweet spots. Her breasts swelled at his touch, and he rewarded them with added attention, squeezing, caressing, teasing until her nipples tightened into pebble-hard buds.

Tracing his mouth over her brows, her closed eyelids, the line of her jaw, he made his way down to suckle those pert tips, making her moan and wriggle beneath him.

She let her knees fall open, pulling him farther into the cradle of her thighs. He came more than willingly, settling against her, rubbing in all the right places.

Soon they were panting, writhing, clawing each other like wild animals. With a strangled groan, Alex grasped her waist, sitting back as he tugged her up to straddle his hips. Her arms tightened around him, her nails raking his skin.

The flats of his hands swept up either side of her spine,

sliding under her hair to cup the back of her skull. His fingers massaged, then dug in as he captured her mouth.

Long minutes ticked by while the only sounds in the room were their mingled breaths, their bodies moving together and the staccato interruption of deep growls and desperate moans.

Even though she was perched inches higher than Alex, he was definitely driving their passion. Which was fine, since he was really, *really* good at it. But she didn't want to be just a passenger on this bus, passively riding along wherever he decided to take them.

She wanted to *drive,* baby, and show him that a resort cleaning lady could blow his socks off just as easily as some silver-spoon socialite strumpet. Better, even, since she didn't give a flip about messing up her hair.

Bracing her legs on either side of him, she gripped his shoulders and pushed, toppling him backward and coming to rest over him with a satisfied smirk on her face. He returned her smile with a grin of his own, letting her know he was just as game for this position as any other.

"A take charge kind of woman," he said, running his hands along her torso until they cupped her breasts. His thumbs teased the undersides, coming just close enough to her nipples to make her bite her bottom lip in longing. "I like it."

Well, then, he should *love* her. She'd been taking charge of her life for as long as she could remember—to her parents' continued consternation. Even before it had become a necessity, Jessica had been more headstrong than was probably wise. Lord knew, it had gotten her into trouble on more than one occasion. She only hoped tonight wouldn't prove to be the biggest mistake of them all.

"So you're in charge," Alex told her, breaking into her fractured thoughts. His thumbs were growing bolder, finally brushing the very tips of her oversensitized breasts, causing them to grow almost painfully tight. "What's next?"

That pesky act-before-you-think gene had backfired on her again. Because her liberal, uninhibited streak seemed to have abandoned her, along with all the strength in her limbs. She no longer wanted to tower over him, but thought she would be better off sinking into the bedclothes in a pile of boneless flesh and nerve endings. That's what Alex's touch did to her—turned her to mindless, quivering mush.

But she needn't have worried. Alex might *say* he liked a strong-willed, take-charge woman—at least in bed—but he had no problem taking the reins when necessary. Abandoning her breasts, he splayed his palms at her waist and down her hips. Raising her slightly, he centered her over his burgeoning erection, brushing lightly between her folds with just the tip.

Jessica sucked in a breath, and Alex bared his teeth, nostrils flaring. Taking her hands, he wrapped them firmly around his hardened length. He was hot to the touch, soft velvet over tempered steel and throbbing beneath her fingers.

"Take me," he told her through gritted teeth. "Show me what you want, how you want it."

How could she resist? He was like a holiday buffet and she was a very hungry reveler.

Angling her hips just so, she brought him flush with her center. Then slowly…slowly, slowly, slowly…she sank down. Inch by inch he filled her, and the feeling was exquisite. To him, too, she guessed, judging by his long, low moan of satisfaction. His eyes fluttered closed, his hands clutched at her hips and beneath her rear, his thighs were as tense as iron beams.

She, however, was loose, almost liquid. Warmth spread through her veins, filled her belly, and surrounded him with moisture where they were connected. His body jerked, driving him higher inside of her, causing her internal muscles to spasm in response.

Though he was still breathing heavily, still holding himself gallantly in check, he smiled up at her, blue eyes flashing with devilish intent.

Oh, my. How had she resisted him for so long? Granted, their "relationship" had pretty much moved at the speed of light as it was. But gazing down at him now, knowing that he was not only movie-star handsome, but oozed sophistication and charm from every pore, she wondered how she hadn't fallen at his feet the very first day—first moment— they'd met. How every woman he came in contact with didn't simply drop to the nearest surface flat on her back like an upturned beetle.

That was the power he possessed—at least over her. He had the power not only to seduce her with barely a whisper, but wipe every ounce of sense straight out of her head.

What they were doing here tonight, in this room, in this bed, had nothing to do with good judgment and everything to do with pure, raw, primal instinct and desire.

Tossing her head from side to side, she shook her hair back over her shoulders and wriggled atop him to find just the right position. Alex growled, fingers digging into her flesh, and tensed even more between her thighs.

"Don't do that unless you're ready to relinquish control," he warned in something akin to a hiss, "because I'm about two seconds from rolling you over and finishing this, whether you like it or not."

A shiver rolled down her spine at his deep-throated threat. Oh, she suspected she would like that very much, indeed. She was tempted to say *yes, please* and let him do just that.

But staying in charge—at least for a while longer—was the only way she knew she'd be able to look herself in the mirror tomorrow. She wanted no doubts, no cracks in the story she might tell herself that would allow her to alter facts. She didn't want to wake up with enough doubts to convince herself that he'd taken advantage of her.

No, she wanted to be sure that if guilt was going to set in, it would rest squarely on her own shoulders. And that if anyone—especially anyone in her family, such as Erin—ever found out, she wouldn't give them further reason to paint Alexander Bajoran as a bad guy.

Running her tongue across her lip—slowly...from one side to the other...first the top...then the bottom—she watched his pupils dilate and his chest hitch with his ragged breathing.

"Poor baby," she murmured in her best sex kitten voice. "Am I being too rough on you?"

On the word *rough,* she flexed the inner walls of her feminine channel, squeezing him like a vise.

He moaned.

"Making this too...*hard?*"

She flexed again, this time coming up on her knees so that the friction, the rasping of their flesh drew sparks, sending currents of electricity outward to shock them both.

He groaned, snarled, muttered a colorful oath. And Jessica grinned at the knowledge that if their social circumstances were reversed—if they'd been doing this five years ago while her family still had control of their company—she could probably have gotten *him* to sign his company over to *her.*

That feeling of superiority, though, was short-lived. While he lifted off the bed and she continued to cant her hips back and forth in a slow, methodical motion, Alex reached for her breast again with one hand. To rub and squeeze and caress. He tweaked her nipples, making her shudder. Then, when it was her turn to let her eyes slide closed, he dropped his other hand between her legs and found the secret, swollen bud sure to send her spiraling out of control.

She moaned, biting her tongue until she thought she might draw blood, as ecstasy built to an almost unbearable pressure inside of her.

Alex stared at Jessica, fighting his own need to moan, possibly even whimper. Had he ever seen a woman so beautiful? Ever met anyone quite like Jessica Madison? He'd never gone to bed with one, of that he was certain.

He couldn't explain his overwhelming attraction to her, but he was sure as hell grateful for it—as well as her mutual enthusiasm. If she'd turned him down out there on the balcony, walked away after only a single too-brief kiss, he suspected he'd have spent the rest of the night taking out his frustrations by trying to punch a hole in one of the suite's walls with his forehead.

But she hadn't turned him down. She'd turned him *on,* then stuck around to do something about it.

Her skin was alabaster silk, running like water under his fingertips. Her mouth was equally soft: warm and inviting and sweeter than anything he'd ever tasted.

And the rest of her... He didn't think words had yet been invented to describe the rest of her. How she moved with him and around him. How she welcomed him and made him want to cherish her and ravish her both at the same time. How her hazel eyes turned dark and liquid when she looked at him. They were so wide and inviting, he thought he could drown in them without a single regret.

Those weren't exactly the thoughts he wanted to be thinking about a one-night stand, but they were there all the same.

And then he couldn't think at all because she was moving on him like sin itself. Long, sure strokes that drove him deeper. Made his jaw lock and his eyes roll back in his head.

He clutched her hips tight enough to leave bruises and had to make a concerted effort to loosen his hold before he did. Not that Jessica seemed to notice. Her straight white teeth were locked on her lower lip...her lashes trembled like butterfly wings as she struggled to keep her eyes open while passion coaxed them closed...and her pace never faltered as she undulated above him.

His own hips rose and fell with her movements, meeting her stroke for stroke, thrusting as deeply as possible and trying for more. Her hands flexed and curled on his chest until her nails dug into the muscles like claws and then released as she reached up to cup her breasts.

The sight of those slender fingers with their neatly trimmed but unmanicured nails curving over her soft, cushiony flesh, touching herself, bringing herself added pleasure, nearly sent him over the edge. Then she tweaked her nipples, arched her spine, and threw her head back on a rich-as-hundred-year-old-scotch moan, and he knew he was a goner.

In one sharp, fast motion, he flipped her to her back, drawing a yelp of surprise from those pink, swollen, delectable lips. Rising over her, he shifted her legs to his waist, encouraged when she linked them together at the base of his spine, heels digging in.

"Hold on, sweetheart." The endearment slipped past his lips before he could stop it, but he couldn't say he regretted it, not when her grip tightened around him, both inside and out.

"Yes," she gasped when he began to pound into her. Long, sure strokes, as deep as he could go to bring them both to the keenest, highest peak of satisfaction.

He moved faster, thrusting in time with her rapid-fire murmurs of *yesyesyesyesyes* until the world tilted, an invisible surf crashed in his ears and everything washed away to nothing except the woman beneath him and the startling, intense, overwhelming pleasure rocketing through him like a meteor crashing to earth.

When he came down, Jessica was breathing rapidly against him, her body splayed on the mattress in proverbial rag-doll fashion.

Well, wasn't he a heel. He'd enjoyed himself to the nth degree, but hadn't bothered to make sure she'd reached her completion first. So much for being a gentleman.

Then she lifted her gaze to his, arms going around his neck while her fingers combed through his hair near the nape. And she smiled.

"Better than dessert," she said just above a whisper.

Blowing out a relieved breath, he returned her grin before leaning in for a soft, lingering kiss. "Who says we can't have both?"

Six

Jessica had been right about the resort's desserts—they were delicious.

So how scary was it that she hadn't enjoyed that indulgence nearly as much as getting naked and rolling around with Alex?

Three times.

After that first amazing encounter, they'd only made it to the bathroom for a quick potty break before somehow ending up back in bed, getting sweaty all over again.

An hour after that, Alex had regained enough strength to reach for the phone and call for room service. She'd told him it wasn't necessary, that she wasn't even particularly hungry anymore. At least not for food.

But he'd insisted. The dishes had been preordered, so the kitchen was simply waiting for his call to send them up. Besides, he'd said, no dinner date was complete without dessert.

She thought heart-stopping, pulse-pounding, coma-inducing sex probably qualified as a decent substitute.

The fruits and pastries, crèmes and sauces that he'd spooned and then hand-fed her had been pretty yummy, too, though. She'd especially enjoyed the bits he'd eaten off her bare skin, and then let her lick off his.

Which had led to that third and final incredible experience that had started on the sitting room sofa...and somehow ended on the very desk she'd snooped through earlier.

Afterward he'd picked her up and carried her back to bed. Good thing, since she'd been doing her best impression of a jellyfish by that point.

She'd drifted off, tucked snuggly against Alex's solid warmth, his strong arm holding her close. And for a while she'd let herself pretend.

That it meant something.

That what they'd shared had a longer shelf life than expired milk.

That she wasn't deceiving him and he hadn't ruined her family.

But all too soon she came awake, reality slapping her hard across the face. Careful not to disturb him, she'd slipped from the bed, from his arms, and gathered her clothes, dressing as quickly and quietly as possible.

Tiptoeing from the bedroom, she moved through the sitting room, praying she could find her purse and get out before Alex noticed she was missing. Then she saw his briefcase, lying open on the coffee table. Frozen midstride, she stood staring at it, battling with herself over what to do next.

Should she turn around and leave, as she'd planned, ignoring the blatant invitation to snoop just a little more? Or should she peek, check to see if there was anything even remotely incriminating inside?

She felt like a dieter standing over a plate of fresh-baked chocolate chip cookies. Tempted. So very tempted.

With a quick glance toward the open bedroom door, she decided to risk it. Rushing forward, she put her clutch down beside the case and started riffling through the papers and manila folders.

It was too dark to see much, her eyes adjusting as best they could to the bit of moonlight shining through the French doors leading to the balcony.

As far as she could tell, it was more of what she'd found in the nightstand. Interoffice memos, contract notations, design sketches. Nothing worthy of fueling Erin's proposed plan of corporate espionage.

Then, at the very bottom of the case, she spotted one final packet. Not a plain manila folder, but a darker manila envelope stamped with giant red block letters she couldn't have missed, even if the room had been pitch-black: CONFIDENTIAL

Jessica's heart stopped. It was sealed. Well, tied closed with a thin red string, at least. But it was obviously private, not meant to be viewed by anyone but Alex and other authorized Bajoran Designs personnel.

Sparing another glimpse toward the bedroom, she took a deep breath and hurried to untie the stringed closure.

She didn't know what she'd been expecting...a treasure map or stack of secret security codes, maybe. Or maybe that was just her vivid imagination, replaying various scenes from her favorite action-adventure movies in her head while she pretended to be a poor man's Indiana Jones.

But what she found was no more surprising than anything else she'd stumbled upon so far. A stack of papers labeled Proposed Princess Line, with sketches of a dozen or so fresh designs included. They were for earrings, necklaces and rings, all in matching sets with similar design elements.

Obviously these were suggested pieces for a new line Bajoran Designs intended to launch in the near future. Likely a multimillion-dollar business venture.

Jessica couldn't have said what possessed her, but before she even realized what she was doing, she set the envelope under her clutch and replaced the other papers and folders inside the briefcase, making sure to leave it open exactly as she'd found it.

She was tired and maybe not thinking straight. But she would take the proposed designs with her to study more carefully in the safety of her apartment, and decide then whether or not to show them to her cousin.

With luck she could sneak them back into Alex's briefcase in the morning when she cleaned his room, long before he even noticed they were gone.

Pushing to her feet, she grabbed her purse and the envelope and rushed to the door, careful not to make a sound as she slipped out of Alex's suite, leaving him sleeping peacefully and hopefully none the wiser.

Seven

One Year Later

Alexander made his way down the hall toward his office with his nose buried in the company's latest financials. Not bad for a year when the country's economy was pretty much in the toilet, but he suspected they would have done better if someone else hadn't gotten the scoop on their Princess Line.

A deep scowl marred his brow. It had taken him a while to figure out, but now he knew exactly who was responsible for that little betrayal, too.

He was digging into his anger, mentally working up a good head of steam, when a peculiar sound caught his attention. Pausing midstride, he tilted his head to listen. Heard it again.

The unfamiliar noise seemed to be coming from the conference room he'd just passed. Backing up a few steps, he glanced through the open doorway.

His arms, along with the papers he was holding, fell to his sides. He blinked. Shook his head and blinked again.

He knew what he was seeing, and yet there was a part of his brain that refused to function, that told him it couldn't be what he thought it was. Obviously he was imagining things… but did illusions usually come with full surround sound?

The noise he'd heard earlier came again. This time he identified it easily, mainly because the source of that sound was sitting right in front of him.

In the center of the long conference table that was normally filled with high-ranking Bajoran Designs' employees sat a white plastic crescent-shaped carrier. And in the carrier, lined with bright material covered in Noah's ark cartoon animals, sat a baby.

A baby.

In his boardroom.

While the child continued to kick his legs and coo, Alex double-checked to be sure the room was empty. It was. No mother or father or grandparent or nanny in sight.

Stepping out of the room, he looked in both directions up and down the hall. It was completely deserted.

Since this was the floor where his office was located, it tended to be quiet and not heavily trafficked. Just the way he liked it. The majority of Bajoran Designs' employees were stationed on other floors of the building.

But that didn't mean someone wasn't visiting, child in tow. He couldn't say he thought much of their parenting skills, considering they'd left what looked to be their months-old infant completely unattended on a tabletop.

"Rose!" he shouted down the hall toward his personal assistant's workstation. He couldn't see her from where he was standing, but knew she would be there. She always was. "Rose!"

"Where's the fire?" she asked in an exasperated voice, coming into sight as she headed his way.

He ignored her tone. Having worked together for years, they knew each other better than some husbands and wives. He might be demanding and short-tempered at times, but Rose was twenty years his senior and only let him get away with so much before putting her foot down.

Rather than responding to her question, he pointed a finger and asked one of his own. "What is *that?*"

Rose paused beside him in the doorway, blinked once and said, "It's a baby."

"I *know* it's a baby," he snapped. "What is it *doing* here?"

"Well, how should I know?" Rose replied, equally short. "*I* didn't put it there."

A beat passed while Alex ground his teeth and struggled to get his growing outrage under control.

This was getting him nowhere. His secretary might be a woman, but she apparently wasn't teeming with maternal instincts.

Fine. He would handle the situation himself.

Stalking forward, he turned the baby carrier slightly to face the child head-on. Cute kid. Alex couldn't say he—or she—was any more or less cute than any other baby he'd ever seen, but then, he didn't pay much attention to children one way or another. They were—in his opinion—smelly, drippy, noisy things, and he didn't know why anybody would want or purposely set out to have one of their own.

Which still didn't explain why somebody had left *this one* in his conference room.

The baby smiled and blew a tiny spit bubble as it kicked its feet, sending the carrier rocking slightly. That's when Alex noticed the piece of paper tucked beneath the safety strap holding the infant in place.

Careful not to touch the baby any more than necessary, he removed the paper, unfolded it and read.

Alex—
I know this will come as a shock, but Henry is your son. I'm sorry I didn't tell you about him before now, but please don't hold that against him.
    As much as I love him, I can't keep him with me any longer. He deserves so much more than I can offer right now.
    Please take care of him. And no matter how you feel about me, please tell him that I love him very much and never would have left him if I'd had a choice.

It was signed simply "Jessica."

Jessica. Madison? Mountain View Jessica Madison?

The timing was right, he would admit that much. And he hadn't forgotten a single thing about their encounter, despite the year that had passed since she'd sneaked out of his hotel room—his bed—in the middle of the night.

A muscle ticked in his jaw as he clamped his teeth together more tightly than nine out of ten dentists would probably recommend.

She'd left without a word, which was bad enough. But it wasn't until later, much later, that he'd discovered the proposed designs for his company's Princess Line were also missing.

It hadn't taken more than three seconds for him to realize she'd taken them. That she'd apparently been some kind of spy, either sent by a competing corporation or come on her own to ferret out Bajoran Designs secrets.

And she'd found herself a doozy, hadn't she? He might be CEO of the family business, but it had been none too comfortable standing in front of the Board of Directors and explaining that he'd lost the Princess Line prospectus. Not just lost them, but had them stolen out from under him by what he could only assume was the competition.

Not that he'd told them the whole truth. He hadn't wanted to admit that he'd let himself be seduced and then robbed. He'd also hoped to get to the bottom of the theft on his own before coming totally clean. Which is why he'd talked them out of taking legal action or filing an insurance claim.

But he'd seethed for months. And though no one had said anything to his face—no one would dare, unless they had a death wish as well as a desire to be on the unemployment line—he knew he'd lost a certain amount of respect from his colleagues.

He wasn't sure which bothered him more—that, the loss of revenue for the company or his apparent gullibility at the hands of a beautiful woman.

Now, just when he'd finally begun to get his impromptu affair with Jessica the Chambermaid-slash-Evil Seductress out of his system and memory banks enough to focus more fully on the theft itself, here she was again. Popping into his life and claiming he'd fathered her child.

Not a single fiber of his being told him he could believe the note in his hand. If it was even from Jessica…or the woman he'd known as Jessica. After all, he had no proof that was her real name. Or that she'd actually written this letter…or that this was really her child…or that this was really *his* child.

Even so, he found himself studying the infant's features. Was there any hint of himself there? Any hint of Jessica?

"Call security," he told Rose without bothering to look in her direction. "Tell them to search the building for anyone who doesn't belong—especially a lone woman."

A lone woman with a streak of wild blue in her blond hair and eyes the color of smoky quartz. He thought the words, but didn't speak them.

"I also want to see the video footage from this floor."

Wrapping his fingers firmly around the handle of the carrier, he lifted the child off the table and marched away, certain his orders would be followed to the letter.

"I'll be in my office."

What the *hell* was he supposed to do with a baby?

At the moment, he was pacing a hole in the carpet of his home office, bouncing the squealing, squalling infant against his chest and shoulder. He still wasn't convinced this was his son, but the evidence certainly did point in that direction.

Security had searched Bajoran Designs' entire building—including the floors and offices that had no affiliation with the company. Nothing.

Then they'd reviewed the security tapes from Alex's floor, as well as the building's main entrance. Sure enough, there had been a woman who rang all kinds of bells and whistles for him.

She'd been wearing sunglasses and a knit cap pulled down over her ears, the collar of her denim jacket flipped up to cover as much of her features as possible. But her attempts at anonymity couldn't conceal the blond curls peeking out from beneath the cap, the high cheekbones holding up the shades or those lips that reminded him of sinful, delightful things better shared in the dark of night.

So while he couldn't say with one hundred percent certainty that the woman on the security tapes—toting a baby carrier on the way in but not on the way out—was the Jessica he knew from Mountain View Lodge, it was sure as hell looking that way. Which meant this *could* be his child.

According to Rose's best nonmaternal guess, she pegged the infant to be three or four months old. And given that he'd spent the night with the child's alleged mother a year ago… Yeah, the timing was more right than he cared to contemplate.

The question was: What did he do now?

Rose had been no help whatsoever. She'd told him to get himself some diapers and formula, and then take the baby out of the office because his coos—which were headed much more toward fussing by that point—were getting on her nerves.

Not having a better game plan, he'd done just that. Called his driver and ordered him to stop at the nearest grocery store on the way home.

Normally, he'd have sent his housekeeper out for baby supplies—and he probably still would. But at that very moment, he'd somehow known that he shouldn't wait much longer to have food for this kid's belly and clean Pampers on his bottom. Babies, he was quickly learning, were both demanding and smelled none too fresh after a while.

Thank God a clerk had come to his aid and pointed out a dozen items she insisted he couldn't do without. He'd been in no position to argue, so he'd bought them all.

No matter how rich he was, however, he learned the hard way that he couldn't snap his fingers and get a nanny to appear on his doorstep within the hour. He'd tried—asked Mrs. Sheppard to call every nanny placement agency in the city and offer whatever it took to have someone at his estate that night. She'd run into nothing but one stone wall after another.

No one was available on such short notice, and even if they had been, the agencies insisted he had to go through the official hiring process, which included filling out applications and running credit and background checks. He'd gotten on the phone himself and tried to throw his weight around in a way he rarely did, but suspected that had simply bumped him to the bottom of their waiting lists.

In a growing series of things that were just not going in

his favor today, it turned out Mrs. Sheppard was no more maternal than Rose. The minute she'd spotted him walking through the door carrying a whimpering child, she'd scowled like a storm cloud and firmly informed him with more than a hint of her usual Irish lilt that she "didna do babies," hadn't signed on to care for children and wasn't paid well enough to start now.

He *paid* her well enough to care for every child who passed through the gates of Disneyland on a daily basis, but understood her point. Until today he "didn't do babies," either.

Maybe that's why all of the people in his employ were less willing to volunteer for child-care duty than he was. Having an aversion to infants himself, he'd apparently hired staff who felt the same.

Which had worked perfectly well up to now. Suddenly, though, he wished he'd surrounded himself with more of the ticking-biological-clock types. A few women who couldn't wait to take a crying baby off his hands and work whatever natural magic they possessed to restore peace and quiet to his universe.

Before running out for a few more things he thought he might need before morning, Mrs. Sheppard had at least helped him stumble his way through his first diaper change and bottle preparation. He'd gotten the baby—Henry…the child's name was Henry, so he'd better start remembering it—fed and thought he was in the clear.

Still in the little rocking seat with the handle that made for easier toting around, the baby had started to drift off, eyes growing heavy as his tiny mouth tugged at the bottle's nipple like…well, like something he had no business thinking in the presence of an infant. Especially if that infant turned out to be his son and the image in his head was of the child's mother.

And then, just a few minutes after he'd emptied the bottle of formula, Baby Henry had jerked awake and started screaming at the top of his lungs. Alex had rocked the baby seat…shushed him in a voice he'd never used before in his life…and tried every trick he could think of—which weren't many, he was frustrated to realize.

Finally, having run out of options, he'd lifted the child from the padded seat and tucked him against his chest.

Surprised by his own actions, he'd begun patting the baby's back and bouncing slightly as he crossed the room. Back and forth, back and forth, back and forth in an effort to soothe the bawling child.

He didn't know where any of this came from, but it seemed the natural thing to do. Not that it was working. The baby was sobbing so hard, his little chest was heaving and his breaths were coming in hiccuping gasps.

If this lasted much longer, Alex was going to dial 9-1-1. It was the only option he could think of, given that he had no nanny and no personal knowledge of child rearing. Especially if it meant the difference between being thought a fool for overreacting or letting the poor kid suffocate on his own tears.

He was headed for the phone, intent on doing just that, when the doorbell rang. Halting in his tracks, he took a second to wonder who it could be at this hour—he wasn't expecting anyone except Mrs. Sheppard, and she had her own key—before Henry gave another hitching sob, driving him to action. Whoever it was, he hoped to hell they knew something, *anything* about babies.

Please, God, let this be Mary Poppins, he thought as he stalked out of his office and across the gleaming parquet foyer.

Yanking the door open, he jerked to a stop, shock reverberating through his system.

The person standing on the other side of the threshold was better than Mary Poppins…it was the baby's mother.

Jessica.

Eight

Jessica's heart was pounding like the bass of a hard rock ballad in her chest, tears pouring down her face. Coming here hadn't been part of the plan. And the last thing she'd intended was to knock on the front door.

But she couldn't stand it anymore. Henry's sobs were tearing her apart, causing a deep, throbbing physical pain that couldn't be ignored one second longer.

She'd been crying since she'd sneaked into Alex's office and left her sweet little baby on his boardroom table. No choice, nowhere else to turn.

She'd done everything she could on her own, and finally realized that turning Henry over to his father was the only option left unless she wanted to raise her child in a homeless shelter.

But doing the right thing, the *only* thing, didn't mean she could just walk away. She'd left Henry with a note for Alex to discover, praying he would believe her words and accept the baby as his son. That he would love and care for him the way their son deserved.

Then she'd sneaked back out of the building, but had stood across the street, waiting and watching. And crying. Crying so hard, she'd been afraid of attracting unwanted attention.

When she'd spotted Alex coming out of the building to meet his car at the curb, baby carrier balanced at his hip, her pulse had spiked. She'd taken it as a good sign, though, that he'd had the baby with him. And that he hadn't called the police to turn her in as an unfit mother, as well as for child abandonment.

She hadn't known where he was going, though, and suddenly she'd *needed* to know. Not that she could afford to hail a cab, and she'd sold her own car months ago.

With no other options, she'd taken a chance, using public transportation, then walking the rest of the way to Alex's estate. A gorgeous, sprawling sandstone mansion on fifteen private, perfectly landscaped acres in an area she was well familiar with from her own time living in Seattle.

It was also gated, but she'd lucked out—huffing and puffing from the uphill climb, she'd reached the entrance to Alex's property just as someone else had been leaving. The car had pulled out, turning onto the main road, and Jessica had slipped through the iron gate as it was slowly swinging closed.

Then she'd rounded the house, looking in every window she could reach until she'd spotted Alex and Henry. Heart in her throat, she'd used a less-than-sturdy hedge as a stepping stool, standing on tiptoe to watch. Just…watch.

She'd wanted so badly to go inside and hold her baby. To take him back and tell Alex it had all been a horrible mistake. But even if she had…even if it *was*…her circumstances would be exactly the same.

No choice. She had no choice.

It was when Henry had started crying—sobbing, really—and had refused to be calmed, that she couldn't stand it any longer. She wanted her baby, and he obviously needed her.

So here she stood, face-to-face with the one man she'd had no intention of ever being face-to-face with again.

She didn't know what to say to him, so she didn't mince words. "Give him to me," she said, plucking the baby out of his grasp.

She wasn't the least bit familiar with the layout of the house, but she didn't particularly care. Moving across the foyer, she headed in the direction she thought would take her to Alex's spacious office den. The one she'd been hiding outside of for the past half hour, spying on her child and ex-lover.

Pulling off her knit cap and shrugging out of her jacket—one arm at a time while balancing Henry in the other—she tossed them aside, bringing the baby even closer to her chest, tucking him in and crooning. From the moment he heard her voice, he began to relax.

It took what seemed like forever for his cries to die down, but she continued to sway, hum, pat him on the back. She whispered in his ear, telling him in a low, singsong voice how much she loved him, how sorry she was for leaving, and that everything would be okay. She wasn't sure she believed it, but she promised all the same.

A long time later, his tiny body stopped shuddering and she knew he was sleeping, his face turned in to her neck, his warm breath fanning her skin.

It was the most amazing sensation, one she hadn't thought she'd get to experience again anytime soon…if ever. Her own chest grew tight, moisture gathering behind her closed eyelids.

As much as she was trying to absorb every precious moment, she knew she was also stalling. Because Alex was standing behind her. Watching and waiting and likely fuming with fury.

She couldn't hide behind the baby forever, though. Time to pay the piper.

On a sigh, followed by a deep, fortifying breath, Jessica turned.

She'd been right. Alex was standing only a few feet away, arms crossed, blue eyes as cold as a glacier glaring at her. That look cut through her, chilling her to the bone.

Swallowing hard, she kept her voice low to avoid waking the baby, hoping Alex would take the hint and do the same.

"I'm sorry," she told him. "I shouldn't have abandoned him like that."

Abandoned. God, that made her sound like such a bad mother. But it was the truth, wasn't it?

She expected him to jump on that, throw all kinds of nasty accusations at her—though in a subdued tone, she hoped.

Instead, he pinned her in place with a sharp, angry stare. "Is he mine?"

"Yes," she answered simply. Honestly. "His middle name is Alexander, for you. Henry was my grandfather's name."

Without responding to that bit of information, he asked, "Are you willing to take a blood test to prove it?"

It hurt to have him ask, but she wasn't surprised. She'd lied to him—so many times, about so much…things he didn't even know about yet, let alone the things he did.

"Yes," she murmured again.

That seemed to give him pause. Had he expected her to refuse?

She wasn't exactly perched soundly on the higher ground, here. She had no room to complain and no right to be offended. If there were hoops he wanted her to jump through, and punishments he wanted to dole out, she had no choice but to acquiesce.

"I'll make an appointment first thing in the morning."

She nodded, though she knew he neither needed nor was waiting for her to agree.

"You'll stay here tonight," he continued, his tone brooking no argument. "In fact, you'll stay here until I know what's going on and have decided what to do about it."

As uncomfortable a prospect as that was, she was oddly okay with it. It wasn't as if she had anywhere else to go. Even after leaving Henry at Alex's office, her only plan had been to look for work here in Seattle or catch a bus back to Portland and try to find something there, but she suspected she probably would have ended up sleeping in the bus terminal instead. Provided Alex didn't intend to lock her in a dungeon somewhere in this giant house of his, it might be nice to sleep in a real bed for a change.

When she offered no resistance to his demands, he tipped his head and moved toward the door. "Follow me." He didn't look back, assuming—or rather, *knowing*—she would do exactly as he said.

Still holding a sleeping Henry, she trailed him out of the office, across the cavernous foyer and up a wide, carpeted stairwell to the second floor. He led her down a long hallway lined with what she could only assume was priceless artwork and credenzas topped with fresh-cut flowers in crystal and Ming-style vases.

Stopping suddenly, he pushed open one of the doors and stood aside for her to pass. It was a beautiful, professionally decorated guest room, complete with queen-size four-poster canopy bed and private bath. Done in varying shades of sage-green, it was unisex; not too masculine or too feminine.

"If you try to leave," Alex said from behind her, "I'll stop you. If you try to take my child from me—if he really is my child—I'll have both the police and my attorneys on you faster than you can blink."

She had no doubt he was rich enough, powerful enough and bitter enough to carry through with the threat. While she was broke, powerless and too exhausted to walk much farther, let alone attempt to run away.

Turning to face him, she continued to rub the baby's back. "I'm not going anywhere, Alex. I handled this badly, and for that, I apologize. This isn't how you should have found out you're a father. So whatever you need me to do…within reason," she added with a raised brow, "well, I figure I owe you one."

His raised brow told her he thought she owed him more than just one. And maybe he was right. But her response seemed to reassure him. Some of the tension went out of his shoulders and the lines bracketing his mouth lessened a fraction.

"Tell me what you need for him."

His eyes darted to Henry and she *thought* she saw a hint of softness there. Although she might have imagined it.

She had next to nothing. By the time she'd decided leaving Henry with Alex was her last resort, she'd been out of formula and down to her last diaper. If she hadn't, she probably wouldn't have been able to go through with it.

She could have gone to her parents, but that was still a can of worms she was trying to avoid opening. And the guilt of not alerting Alex to the fact that he was a father had started to eat at her, so she'd decided that he was a better "last resort."

"Everything," she said dejectedly.

"Make a list," he told her. "My housekeeper is picking up a few things right now. I'll try to catch her and have her get whatever else you need while she's out."

Jessica nodded, expecting him to go…unless he intended to pull up a chair and stand guard at the door all night. Instead, he remained rooted to the spot, his features drawn in contemplation.

"Will this be all right for him?" he finally asked. His arms swept out to encompass the room. "I don't have a crib or anything else...nursery-ish."

She offered a small smile. As angry as he was, he was still concerned about his son's safety and comfort. She found that endearing. And it gave her hope that his resentment would one day give way to understanding.

"We'll be fine," she assured him. "Henry can sleep in the bed with me, and I'll use pillows around the edges to keep him from rolling off."

He considered that for a moment, then said, "I'll make arrangements for someone to come by tomorrow and baby proof the place. Make a list for that, too—whatever you and Henry will need for an extended stay, and whatever needs to be done to keep him safe."

She wasn't sure what he meant by that. How *extended* a stay did he have in mind?

But now wasn't the time to question him. She was on thin enough ice as it was.

"We still have to talk," he informed her. "But you look tired, and I know he is. It can wait until tomorrow."

With that, he turned on his heel and walked out, closing the door behind him.

Jessica let out a breath, wishing it was one of relief. Instead, it was only...a short reprieve. As she set about readying the room, herself and the baby for bed, she felt as though a noose was hanging over her head.

Because as bad as today had been...tomorrow promised to be even worse.

Jessica didn't know what time it was when she finally came awake the next morning. Henry had had her up a few times during the night, needing to be changed or fed or simply lulled back to sleep. But she suspected yesterday's stress level had impacted him, as well, because he'd slept like a stone the rest of the time.

Stretching, she glanced beside her to find him awake and smiling around the pacifier in his mouth. His legs were kicking, and when he saw her looking down at him, he waved his arms, too.

"Good morning, sweetheart," she greeted him, unable to resist leaning over and kissing his soft cheek. He made a happy sound from deep in his belly, and she took a minute to blow raspberries on his tummy through his thin cotton T-shirt until he giggled.

Laughing in return, she scooped him up and finally looked at the clock. Ten-thirty. Later than she normally woke, but not quite as late as she'd expected, given the bright sunlight peeking through the drawn floor-to-ceiling curtains. As she started moving around, using the restroom and changing the baby, she heard noises from outside the bedroom door.

Last night, before she'd gone to bed, Alex's housekeeper had arrived with several large fabric totes bulging with baby items. Formula, bottles, pacifiers, toys, onesies, baby lotion, baby shampoo, baby powder…everything. More than Jessica would need to get through just the next few days. And now it sounded as though Alex had a construction crew in the house, building a nursery—or possibly an entire day care center—to his exact specifications.

With Henry at her hip, she opened the door only to find the hallway filled with oversize boxes and shopping bags. She stood rooted to the spot for a minute, stunned and confused.

Noises were coming from next door, and before she could decide which direction to turn—left toward the sounds of the pounding or right toward the stairs—Alex appeared. He strolled down the hall with two men on his heels who were carrying a large, flat cardboard box between them.

"In there," Alex instructed, pointing to the room where all

the building noises were coming from. He waited for them to pass, then waved her ahead of him.

They paused in the doorway of the room beside hers, where several men were busy putting furniture together and attaching shelving to the walls.

"What's all this?" she asked, though she could certainly guess. The half-assembled crib and changing table in the corner were dead giveaways.

"I'm putting a nursery in between our two rooms. That way we'll both be close to the baby in case he needs us during the night."

Jessica swallowed, not quite sure how to respond. Should she be more concerned that Alex's room was apparently only two doors down from where she'd spent last night...or that he seemed to believe she and Henry would be here long enough for a separate nursery to be necessary?

She owed him answers, and, of course, knew that he would want to spend time with his son now that he was aware of Henry's existence, but that didn't mean she—or the baby—were going to stick around forever.

Before she could decide how to respond, he continued.

"I've called Practically Perfect Au Pairs, the premiere nanny agency in the city. They'll be sending potential nannies out over the next few days to be interviewed. You can be there, if you like."

This time she wasn't at a loss for words. Her spine went straight and tight as outrage coursed through her system.

"Henry doesn't *need* a nanny. I'm his mother. I can care for him just fine by myself."

"As evidenced by the fact that you left him in the boardroom of my office building, with a note begging me to take him in," he replied, deadpan.

Jessica's chest squeezed. He was right, and they both knew it. But she'd changed her mind. She was here now, and damned if she'd let him foist her child off on some complete stranger.

"That was yesterday," she told him. "Today, I'm perfectly capable of watching out for my own child. I don't *need* a nanny," she stressed again.

She expected an argument. Worse, she expected him to toss more "unfit mother" accusations at her. Instead, he shrugged one shoulder encased in the fine silk-wool blend of a tailored dark blue suit.

"Humor me," he said in a tone that could only be described as wholly polite. "This is all rather new to me, and I'd feel better having a trained professional on hand for those times when you or I can't be with Henry."

Again the thought crossed her mind that she probably wouldn't be staying with him for long. Certainly not long enough to hire extra staff.

But what she asked him was, "Why wouldn't I be with him?" Her back was still stiff as a rod, her voice carrying more than a hint of wariness.

"We have a lot of ground to cover. You may need a nap after the grilling I plan to give you."

Her eyes widened at that, and suspicion gave way to fear.

"You missed breakfast," he added, jumping so easily from one topic to another that her head started to spin. "But I'm sure Mrs. Sheppard can see that you're fed."

"Oh, that's all right. I don't want to be a both—"

Alex took her elbow, forcibly turning her toward the other end of the house and leading her in that direction.

"Feed the baby," he told her. "Then get yourself something to eat. After that, we'll talk."

He said "we'll talk," but what Jessica heard was, "Let the inquisition begin."

Nine

Alex thought he deserved a damn Academy Award for his performance so far. Every second that he'd been with Jessica, he'd wanted to shake her. Every word that he'd spoken in calm, even tones, he'd wanted to shout at the top of his lungs. It had taken every ounce of control he possessed to hold a normal, mundane conversation with her rather than demand answers. Right there, right now, regardless of how many witnesses might hear.

But he'd bitten his tongue, fisted his hands so tightly he'd nearly drawn blood. Reminded himself that in most situations, one got further by keeping a cool, level head than losing one's temper and raging like a maniac.

As hard as it was to resist turning the full force of his fury on her, he told himself that would only frighten her and possibly cause her to run off again. This time taking *his son* with her.

Oh, there were going to be DNA tests to prove—or disprove—that claim. In addition to the nannies who would be dropping by on and off over the next several days, he had a doctor scheduled to stop in and conduct a paternity test as quickly as possible.

But until he knew for sure, he was going on the assumption that he *was* the child's father. Better safe than sorry, and if he was, he wanted to get a jump on being a dad.

He'd already missed… He didn't know how long. He did know, though, that he'd missed the entire pregnancy, the birth and any number of firsts. First feeding, first diaper change, first time being awakened in the middle of the night and rocking Henry back to sleep.

Alex clenched his teeth until they ached. One more thing to hold against Jessica. The list was getting pretty long.

Biding his time, he led her downstairs to the kitchen and asked Mrs. Sheppard to see to it that Jessica and the baby were both taken care of. Then he'd returned to the foyer to oversee the rest of the baby preparations.

He'd waited thirty minutes. Thirty-two to be exact, before returning to the kitchen, ready to get some answers to the questions burning a hole in his gut.

Walking into the room, he stopped short, taken aback by the sight before him.

Jessica sat at the table of the eat-in nook near the windows, a half-eaten plate of scrambled eggs and toast in front of her. She alternated between taking a bite of her own meal and slipping a spoonful of goopy gray cereal into the baby's mouth. He was perched on her thigh, nestled and in the crook of her arm.

"Why isn't he in the high chair?" Alex asked, his voice reverberating through the room more loudly than he'd intended, startling both Jessica and Henry. He'd ordered the expensive piece of infant furniture, though, so his son should darn well be using it.

Dipping the tiny spoon back into the baby goop, she said, "He's only three months old. He's not quite ready to sit up on his own yet."

Well, there was one question answered. Henry was three months old. The math worked.

He also made a mental note to buy some baby books. He didn't want to learn from Jessica or anyone else what his child could or couldn't do, or what he needed.

Feeling suddenly uncomfortable and slightly self-conscious, he cleared his throat. "When you're finished, come to my office. It's time to get down to business."

As she crossed the front of the house toward Alex's den, Jessica felt for all the world as if she'd been called to the principal's office. Her feet were lead weights and her heart was even heavier. Henry at her hip, in comparison, was light as a feather.

He was also happy today. She shouldn't have been quite so delighted about it, but from the moment she'd arrived last night and plucked him from Alex's arms, Henry had been relaxed and content. Something to be said for her mothering skills, she hoped, as well as their strong mommy/baby bond.

On the heels of that thought, though, came a wave of guilt. She'd had nine months of pregnancy and the three months since Henry was born to bond with him, while Alex had had only yesterday. And that hardly counted, since she'd sprung the baby on him with no warning and hadn't even stuck around to explain.

Which was why she was letting him get away with the strong-arm tactics. He was angry—with good reason. And she was guilty—for bad reasons.

The door was open when she arrived. Alex was seated behind his desk, another man—older and balding—sat in one of the guest armchairs with his back to her.

Alex spotted her almost the moment she stepped inside and stood to greet her.

"Come in," he said, rounding the desk as the other man also got to his feet.

"This is Dr. Crandall," he introduced them, closing the door behind her with a soft click. "Dr. Crandall, this is the young woman I was telling you about."

To Jessica, he added, "Dr. Crandall is here for the paternity test."

Having her integrity called into question stung, but in Alex's shoes she would have insisted on the very same thing. So she extended her arm and shook the doctor's hand.

"Nice to meet you, Doctor."

"You, too, my dear," he said, smiling gently. "And I don't want you to worry about a thing. This is a relatively painless procedure. Just a quick cheek swab, and I should have the results back from the lab by the middle of next week."

"I appreciate that, thank you."

The idea of having Henry's blood drawn hadn't appealed. He'd survived worse, of course, but that still didn't make it a fun prospect.

"Dr. Crandall assures me that the cheek swab tests are just as accurate as blood tests," Alex put in. "The only reason we'd have to have blood drawn later is if the initial tests come back as inconclusive or problematic."

Jessica nodded. "Whatever you need."

Ten minutes later, Alex was walking the doctor to the door, DNA samples labeled and tucked safely into his medical bag. She stood in the doorway of Alex's office, watching as he shook the physician's hand, then ducking back inside before Alex returned.

When he arrived, she was sitting in one of the leather guest chairs, bouncing a giggling Henry on one knee.

Alex stood for a moment, simply watching them. The

woman who'd seared some of the most passionate memories of his life into his brain, and the child they'd most likely made together.

His chest contracted. Without a doubt, he was furious. She'd used him, stolen from him, betrayed him and lied to him. Yet part of him wanted to cross the room, drop to one knee and wrap his arms around them, holding them close and cherishing them the way a family should be cherished.

He wondered what would have happened if his relationship with Jessica had played out differently. If she hadn't spent the night with him simply to steal company secrets. If she'd stuck around instead of running off before the sun rose the next morning so they could share breakfast, get to know each other better, perhaps agree to keep seeing one another.

Alex wasn't a man of fickle emotions, so when he'd awakened that morning after making love with her, looking forward to making love to her again…and possibly again…he'd known he'd found something special. Or thought so, at least. Reality had proven to be quite different.

But deep down, he knew the possibility of a good, old-fashioned romance had existed. They might have dated, shared a short engagement and walked down the aisle before deciding to start a family. Baby Henry would still have been part of the big picture, just a little further down the road.

Fate had a way of turning things upside down, though, then sitting back for a good chuckle at the expense of the humans who had been played with like marionettes.

Which meant he was now faced with fatherhood first and…he didn't know what else second.

Clearing his throat, he strode across the room, returning to his seat behind the desk. It was awkward to put such cold, professional distance between himself and the mother of his child, but he felt comfortable there, and if it intimidated Jessica at all, kept her on the level, then it was the right position to take.

"I think I'm going to need a quick rundown of events," he told her, careful to keep his tone level and unaccusatory. "Why did you take off in the middle of the night? And if Henry is my son, why didn't you contact me when you found out you were pregnant?"

He watched her eyes, saw the pulse in her throat jump as she swallowed.

"It was a one-night stand. I didn't think you'd want me to still be there in the morning," she murmured. "And then when I went back the next day to clean your room, you were gone."

"My business in Portland wrapped up a few days early, and I was needed back here in Seattle. I wanted to ask about you," he admitted—albeit against his better judgment, "or at least leave a note, but was afraid it might get you in trouble."

He very intentionally didn't mention the missing Princess Line prospectus. It was a subject that definitely needed to be discussed, but not now. Not until he knew for certain whether or not Henry was his son.

For the time being, the child and his possible unexpected fatherhood trumped everything else.

She nodded somewhat ruefully. "It probably would have gotten me fired."

Just as he'd suspected. "I called a while later, but whoever I talked to claimed there was no one by the name of Jessica Madison working at Mountain View. And that the only Jessica they'd had on staff had quit the week before."

He'd considered digging deeper, perhaps hiring a private investigator to track her down. But then he'd realized how that would look: desperate. Especially since he hadn't yet hired a P.I. to look into the theft. If their one night together hadn't meant enough to her to make her stick around, then he'd look pretty pathetic chasing after her like a lovelorn pup.

So he'd put her and what he still considered a spectacular intimate experience behind him. Or tried, at any rate. And he'd succeeded at putting her out of his everyday thoughts, if not his late-night, private ones.

"You must have called soon after I discovered I was pregnant," she said.

His mouth turned down in a frown. "You quit because of that?"

A strange look passed over her features, and it took a second for her to reply.

"I had to. It wouldn't have been long until I was unable to keep up with the workload, and the chemicals we used to clean wouldn't have been good for the baby. Besides, the owners of the resort weren't too fond of unwed mothers being on the payroll. They thought it tarnished the resort's pristine reputation and would have come up with a reason to let me go before long."

Alex made a mental note never to stay at Mountain View Lodge again. If anything, single and expectant mothers needed their jobs more than other employees. And considering some of the behavior that often took place at those types of high-scale resorts—adultery topping the list—he didn't think the owners had a lot of room to point fingers.

Getting back to the subject at hand, he said, "Why didn't you tell me when you found out? You knew who I was and where to find me."

It wasn't always easy to get in touch with him—Rose was an excellent guard dog—but if Jessica had left her name and at least a hint of what she needed to talk to him about, he would have returned her call. Hell, he would have relished the chance to see her again—for more reasons than one.

He didn't know how he would have handled the news of her unexpected pregnancy. Probably much the same as he was handling the news of Henry's existence now—with a fair dose of skepticism and trepidation. He liked to think he would have done the right thing, though, once he'd established the veracity of her claim. Much as he was trying to do now.

He was playing it smart, getting medical proof before accepting parental responsibility, but if Henry turned out to be his, he would do more than put a crib in one of the extra guest rooms and make sure his name was on the child's birth certificate. He would be laying full claim, taking whatever steps were necessary to be sure his son stayed with him. Whether Jessica liked it or not.

Why didn't you tell me when you found out you were pregnant?

It was the question Jessica had been dreading ever since she'd made the decision *not* to tell him.

It had been the wrong decision. Or at the very least, the wrong thing to do. There had been so many factors to consider, though, and she'd been so very frightened and alone.

To Alex, however, she said simply, "I didn't think you'd want to know. Most men wouldn't."

A muscle ticked in his jaw, and she got the distinct impression he was grinding his molars together to keep from doing—or saying—something violent.

"I'm not most men," he said slowly and very deliberately, almost as though each word was a statement unto itself. "I would have stepped up to the plate. And I most certainly would have wanted to know I'd fathered a child."

"I'm sorry."

Jessica didn't know what else to say, not without saying far too much. He was angry enough with her already; she didn't think telling him she was a Taylor and that she'd been poking around his hotel room looking for company secrets would do much to improve his mood.

So she kept her mouth shut, knowing he would find out eventually but hoping he would hate her a little less by then.

Ignoring her apology, both physically and verbally, he went on. "If you didn't want me to know about Henry, why did you dump him at my office yesterday?"

She flinched at his less-than-flattering description of her actions, even though that's exactly what she'd done—in his eyes and in her own.

"I didn't feel I had a choice," she told him quietly. "It's been rough being out of work and trying to care for a baby all by myself. I can't find a job until I put Henry in day care, and I can't afford day care until I get a job."

"Don't you have family to turn to? Parents? Relatives who could help you out?"

The short answer was no. The long answer would mean admitting she was a Taylor, and that rather than telling her family she was pregnant by Alexander Bajoran, she'd chosen to run away. Disappear and live one step up from on the streets.

She'd thought so many times about going home and telling her parents everything. But she hadn't wanted to see the disappointment on their faces when they found out who the father of her baby was. Even if she refused to tell them, she was afraid her mother would eventually wear her down and drag the truth out of her.

And if she'd managed to hold out against her mother's badgering, she'd been very much afraid her cousin would come along later and figure it out.

Because Erin knew what she'd been up to in Alex's room at the resort. And she knew that Jessica hadn't been dating anyone around that time. She'd have done the math in her head, become suspicious and started badgering Jessica until she confessed everything. Then Erin would tell Jessica's folks for sure, damn her meddling hide. Her cousin was the impetus behind all of this, yet Jessica was the one to suffer the consequences.

To Alex she said carefully, "No one who could help me out, no."

He considered that for a moment, the tension in his jaw easing slightly. "You should have come to me sooner. *Come* to me," he emphasized. "In person rather than sneaking around like a cat burglar."

"At least I left something instead of stealing something," she quipped in an attempt at levity.

"I'm not sure the authorities would see it that way," he replied with a withering glance that immediately wiped the lopsided smile from her face.

Before the adrenaline from his veiled threat made it into her bloodstream, however, he added, "You were actually pretty good at getting in and out of the building without being seen. How did you manage that?"

"Just lucky, I guess."

If *luck* included practically growing up there while her family was still part of the business, and knowing not only where all the security cameras and blind spots were, but also how the building's security functioned. Or how it *had* functioned, anyway. She'd taken a chance and hoped not much had changed in the past few years.

Alex's eyes narrowed, and she could see the questions swirling there, knew the interrogation wasn't even close to being over. And while he'd certainly earned the right to some answers, she didn't know how much longer she would be able to get away with partial ones and half-truths.

Then as though heaven actually heard her silent pleas, she was saved by the bell. Literally.

From the front of the house the doorbell rang. They heard footsteps, followed by muted voices, and then more footsteps. A minute later there was a soft knock at the office door.

"Come in," Alex called.

Mrs. Sheppard poked her head in. "One of the applicants from Practically Perfect Au Pairs is here," she said.

"Give us two minutes, then show her in," Alex instructed. "Bring us a tray of coffee and hot tea, as well. Thank you."

The housekeeper nodded, pulling the door closed behind her.

"This is only the first interview of many," Alex told Jessica. "Would you like to take Henry off to do something else, or would you like to stay?"

Another woman interviewing for the privilege of taking care of her son when she wasn't readily available? Oh, there was no way she'd leave that decision to anyone else. Not even her baby's father.

Ten

By the end of the day, they'd interviewed half a dozen nannies. They ranged in age from eighteen to probably forty-five or so; college-age girls needing a job and a place to stay while they attended school, to lifelong caregivers. Each of them came with a resumé and the stamp of approval from either Practically Perfect Au Pairs or one of the other professional nanny placement services Alex had contacted.

As nice as most of the people were, though, Jessica found herself balking at the idea of Alex hiring any of them. Credentials, references and background checks aside, none of them seemed quite good enough to be left alone with her child.

She stood in the foyer, waiting while Alex saw the last of the potential nannies out. Shutting the door behind him, he turned to face her.

"So…any possibilities?" he asked, his footfalls echoing on the parquet floor as he crossed to her.

She shrugged a shoulder, not saying anything.

One corner of his mouth quirked up in a half grin. A sexy half grin, she was troubled to note.

Damn him for being so attractive, even when he hated her. And damn herself for still *finding* him attractive when she had so very much to lose at his hands.

"Come on," he cajoled, raising a hand to rub one of Henry's cheeks with the side of his thumb before letting it drop… and stroking her arm with his cupped palm all the way down. The touch made her shiver as goose bumps broke out along her flesh.

"There has to be someone you liked at least a little. You can't be with Henry 24/7, and every child needs a babysitter at some point. So if you had to pick, who would it be?"

Taking a deep breath, she thought back to each of the interviews, the details playing through her memory. One jumped out over all the others.

"Wendy."

His gaze narrowed. "Why?"

"She was friendly and smart," Jessica told him. "And she engaged Henry almost as soon as she walked in. Spoke to him, smiled at him, played with him, split her attention evenly between the three of us. The others seemed more concerned with remaining professional and impressing you."

A beat passed while he digested that. Then he offered a curt nod. "I thought exactly the same thing."

"Really?" Jessica asked, more than a little surprised.

Taking her elbow, he turned her toward the stairs, leading her to the second floor.

"Absolutely. I may not know much about babies, but I do know that a nanny will be spending ninety percent of her time with Henry. Which means that whoever we hire should be more concerned with impressing him, not me."

He smiled at Henry while he spoke, earning himself a giggle and kick, which only made Alex smile wider.

Tweaking the baby's bare toes as they strolled down the hall, he said, "Besides, I noticed the same things you did. She was really quite good with him. I especially liked that she cleaned his toy giraffe with an antibacterial wipe from her purse before handing it back to him after it fell on the floor. All without a hitch in her conversation with us."

"Me, too," Jessica admitted. Actually, she'd loved that part of the interview. Even Jessica's first instinct would have been to simply take her chances that the floor wasn't that dirty, or maybe run the toy under some water if she was near a faucet. The fact that Wendy had come so well prepared before she'd even been hired definitely earned her bonus points.

"So we'll put her at the top of the list," Alex said. "There are still a few more potentials to meet with tomorrow, and then we can decide. But I think we should strike that Donna woman from the pool entirely. She was downright frightening."

Jessica chuckled, even as a shudder stole down her spine. "Definitely. She should be running a Russian prison, not caring for small children and infants."

Alex gave a short bark of laughter. "Maybe I'll mention that to the agency when they ask how the interviews went."

Jessica's eyes widened. "Don't you dare!" she exclaimed, slapping him playfully on the chest with the back of her hand.

She stopped in her tracks, both shocked and horrified at what she'd done. Dear God, what was she thinking? She was joking with him as if they were old friends. Never mind that he held her future in his hands and could decide to punish her in a million alarming ways at the drop of a hat.

She swallowed past the lump in her throat and forced her gaze up to his, an apology on the tip of her tongue. But his expression kept it from going any further.

Rather than looking annoyed or upset, his features were taut, his eyes blazing with something she hadn't seen since their time at the resort. It made her heart skip a beat and sent heat rushing through her system.

Or maybe she was imagining things. Maybe that blaze in his eyes really was annoyance, and she'd amused herself right into a boatload of trouble.

Chest tight, she licked her dry lips and wondered if she could distract him with a change of subject.

"What are we doing up here, by the way?"

For a moment, he continued to stare with that same barely controlled intensity. Then he pulled back just a fraction and gestured behind her.

"The nursery is ready," he said, leading her in that direction. "I thought you might like to see it."

The general decor of the room was the same as it had been before. Pale yellow walls, lacy white curtains at the windows and gleaming hardwood floors. But any original pieces of furniture had been replaced with top-of-the-line baby items.

A spacious oak half-circle crib rested against one wall, a large changing table and storage unit along another, and in the corner sat a beautiful rocking chair she'd be willing to bet was hand carved.

"What do you think?" Alex asked from just over her shoulder.

"It's lovely," she told him. Like something out of *House Beautiful* or *Babies Born with Silver Spoons in Their Mouths*. She was almost afraid to touch anything for fear she'd leave a smudge on the pristine interior. "I can't believe you had all of this done in only one day."

"Getting things done is easy when you have money and know the right people."

A fact she knew quite well from the good old days before Alex had destroyed her family.

"If there's anything else you or the baby need, anything you'd like to change, just say so," he continued. "I want everything to be perfect, and I'm afraid you're my only source of information at the moment where Henry is concerned."

He said it without a hint of censure. At least none that she could detect. But the guilt and underlying threat were there all the same.

"Why are you doing this?" she asked softly. Shifting Henry from one arm to the other, she turned to face Alex more fully. "You don't even know for sure that Henry is yours."

She did, of course, but she'd assumed that was the point of the paternity test they'd taken that afternoon.

Alex shrugged. "Better safe than sorry."

A very simple, off-the-cuff answer, but she suspected there was more to it than that.

"You're going to make us stay, aren't you?" she asked barely above a whisper.

"For the time being," he said without hesitation.

Then, surprising her yet again, he reached out and slid his hands beneath Henry's arms, lifting him out of her grasp and into his own.

For a split second, Jessica held her breath and nearly tried to tug the baby back. She had to remind herself that Alex *was* Henry's father. He *did* have a right to hold him, if he wanted to.

As distant as he'd been up to now, he didn't seem the least bit nervous about it. There was no hesitation, no pause while he considered the best way to position Henry against his thousand-dollar suit.

He was a natural. Either that, or he'd learned on the job during last night's screaming fit. Still, she couldn't resist stretching out a hand to smooth the baby's shirt down his back, making certain everything was just right and he was okay.

It was odd not holding her own baby, not having him almost surgically attached to her side when she was the only person who'd held him for any length of time since he was born. She didn't know what to do with her arms.

Letting them drop to her sides, she dug her hands into the front pockets of her jeans and told herself to leave them there, even though the urge was to fidget like crazy.

As hard as it was to admit, she made herself mumble, "You're really good at that."

"I've been watching you," he said, his gaze meeting and locking with hers. "I figured I should probably get the hang of it if I'm going to be responsible for this little guy from now on."

There it was again, the hint of a threat—or maybe just a reminder—that if Henry was his, Alex intended to exercise his full parental rights.

On the one hand, Jessica was impressed and sort of proud of him for that. A lot of men wouldn't have been the least bit pleased to discover they might have a child they hadn't known anything about.

On the other, she was scared almost spitless at what it might mean for her and Henry. What if Alex tried to take her son away from her? What if he wanted to keep Henry here with him, under his roof, but informed Jessica she was no longer welcome?

Jessica would fight—of course she would. But she already knew her chances were slim to none of winning any kind of battle against a man like Alex, let alone a custody one. Not given his money and influence and her total lack of either, not to mention her past actions and behavior where he was concerned.

Not for the first time she wanted to kick herself for bringing Alex into their lives. She hadn't had a choice; rationally, she knew that. And even more rationally, she knew he had the right to know about and *know* his own child.

But being here, disclosing Henry's existence to Alex, changed everything. It turned their world upside down and shook it like a snow globe.

To make matters worse, Jessica was afraid Henry was already showing signs of being a Daddy's Boy. He was leaning into Alex, completely trusting, completely content. One of his tiny hands was wrapped around Alex's silk tie, likely wrinkling it beyond repair, while his cheek rested on Alex's shoulder, his bow of a mouth working around his pacifier, his fine, light brown lashes fluttering toward sleep.

"He's getting tired," she told Alex, even as her heart cramped slightly at the sight. Until now she'd been the only one to see him get sleepy and doze off. She'd been the only one those miniature fingers had clung to.

"He missed his afternoon nap because of the interviews. We should probably give him a bottle and put him down for a while. If we don't, he's likely to get extremely cranky and keep us both up half the night."

"Only half?"

There was a twinkle of amusement in Alex's blue eyes. One Jessica couldn't help but respond to with a small smile of her own.

"If we're lucky."

Alex nodded. "Why don't you go downstairs for a bottle. I'll stay here with him. While you're down there, tell Mrs. Sheppard we'll be ready for dinner in thirty minutes. You'll join me, I hope."

That caught her off guard. "You're giving me a choice?"

"Of course."

"Would that choice happen to be eat a four-course meal

downstairs with you or enjoy a lovely serving of bread and water alone in my room?"

He chuckled. "My home isn't a prison, and you're not a prisoner."

"Are you sure?" It was a pointed question, one that had her holding her breath while she waited for the answer.

"After the way you've been living, I'd think staying here would almost be a vacation. Why don't you just enjoy it."

As responses went, it wasn't exactly a *You're free to leave anytime you like.* Although he did have a point; staying in this beautiful mansion was a far cry from worrying about where she was going to sleep that night or where her next meal might come from.

And yet she felt just as trapped as she would if he put her in her room and turned the key in the lock on the way out.

"You can't honestly refuse me this," he said when the silence between them had stretched on for several long seconds. "If Henry is my son, as you claim, I've missed the past three months of his life. The *only* three months of his life. I just want to spend some time with him, make up for a bit of that."

When all else fails, throw out a guilt bomb, she thought. And it hit its mark dead center. How could she possibly deny him time with his newly discovered son? Besides, it wasn't as though staying in a million-dollar house on a multimillion-dollar estate was going to be a hardship. Not physically, anyway.

Mentally, there was no telling yet what the toll would be. But she owed him at least this much.

Tipping her head, she kept her thoughts to herself, but let him know he'd won her over by saying, "I guess I'll go down for his bottle, then, and tell Mrs. Sheppard we're almost ready for dinner."

She patted Henry's tiny back, then stepped around them

and headed for the door. Just as she reached it, his voice stopped her.

"You can request bread and water, if your heart is set on it."

Her lips pursed as she fought a grin, but *his* chuckle of amusement followed her halfway down the hall.

Despite the beautiful new nursery just next door, Jessica couldn't bring herself to put Henry down in there for the entire night. He napped in the expensive new crib after his bottle and while Jessica and Alex ate dinner. But even though she left him there as she showered, changed into pajamas and got ready for bed, she hadn't been under the covers for ten whole minutes before leaping back up and marching next door to get him.

She hoped Alex hadn't gone into the nursery during the night to discover what she'd done. Or if he had, that he wouldn't say anything. She didn't feel like explaining her mild case of separation anxiety or the nagging worry that if she didn't have the baby in her sights at all times, Alex might take Henry away from her, hide him from her and never give him back.

Despite those very real concerns, however, Jessica had to admit that Alex had been perfectly pleasant at dinner. She'd been afraid to go down to the dining room with him, afraid to sit across the table from him—just the two of them alone in an almost cavernous room.

She'd expected more of the third degree. Inquisition, Part Two—only this time without the interruption of nanny interviews.

To her surprise and immense relief, he hadn't brought up even one uncomfortable topic of conversation. He'd asked about the baby. A few not-too-personal questions about her pregnancy. Even about where she'd been and what she'd done to support herself before Henry was born. And he'd spoken a bit about how he'd spent that time himself—mostly changes or new developments at Bajoran Designs.

It had actually been almost enjoyable, and she'd flashed back more than once to the only other meal they'd ever shared—that night at the resort. The night she'd let herself be led by her heart and her raging hormones instead of her head. The night Henry was conceived, though neither of them had had a clue about that at the time.

By the time dessert had been served—a simple but delicious fruit tart—he could have asked for her social security number and internet passwords…well, when she'd had use for internet passwords…and she probably would have turned them over as easily as she'd give someone the time of day. She was that comfortable, that lulled into a false sense of security.

But he hadn't. He'd remained a perfect gentleman, seeing her out of the dining room, then asking if she would be all right going back to the nursery and her room on her own while he went to his office to catch up on a bit of work.

It was the ideal opportunity to escape and put some distance between them. That should have made her happy, right? Just being this close to him, under the same roof, was dangerous with a capital *D*.

But she couldn't help feeling just a little disappointed. That what had turned out to be a lovely dinner had come to an end… That her memories of the last time they'd eaten together had been stirred up, warming her, yet leaving her somewhat frustrated by the fact that *this* meal wouldn't be ending the same way…. And possibly even that he wouldn't be accompanying her upstairs to check on Henry and say good-night.

Why she would want Alexander Bajoran to wish her a good-night, she had no idea. It was craziness to even imagine it. If anything she needed him to spend *less* time with her, watch her *less* closely.

In that, her prayers were answered, because he hadn't knocked on her door in the middle of the night to demand she return Henry to the nursery. He wasn't even waiting outside in the hall when she awoke the next morning and stepped out to begin the day.

Jessica did go to the nursery then, changing Henry's diaper and putting him into one of the matching baby-boy outfits Alex had had delivered the day before. He hadn't only ordered items for the baby, either, but had bought a good deal of stuff for her, as well. New clothes and toiletries; even a stack of puzzle books for her bedside table. Ostensibly in case she grew bored—something that rarely happened while caring for a three-month-old infant. Most nights she was asleep before her head hit the pillow.

But Alex's kindness hadn't gone unnoticed.

Henry was his son, a son he had every intention of laying claim to if those paternity tests came back with his name on them. So purchasing things for the boy was to be expected. Maybe not to the extent Alex had gone—"starting small" obviously wasn't a term that existed in his vocabulary—but buying diapers and formula and a few new pieces of clothing was completely within the realm of understanding.

He had absolutely *no* reason to feel the least bit generous toward her, however. He could have stripped the guest room of every creature comfort and left her to wear the same clothes she'd arrived in for the entire stay, and she would have considered it fair punishment for her deceptions.

But he was a bigger man—a kinder, more considerate man—than she could have anticipated. She only wondered how long it would last once he had the confirmation that Henry really was his son. Would he shower her with roses or take back everything and send her packing?

Hitching Henry higher in her arms, she strolled down the carpeted hallway and wide set of stairs, taking a right on her way to the kitchen. It was early yet, with the sun just beginning to cast purplish light through the windows as she passed.

But Henry was an early riser, especially when he was hungry. So she'd get him some cereal and juice, and make sure he was happy before looking for Alex and finding out what was on the agenda for the day. Likely more nanny interviews and questions from his long list of continued demands.

Half an hour later, she was sitting in the breakfast nook with Henry in his baby seat, his face and bib covered in splots of sticky and drying cereal. Mrs. Sheppard bustled around the center island, readying items for the meal she was about to prepare while Henry kicked his feet and sent the plastic seat rocking on the tabletop with every bite.

Jessica couldn't help grinning at her child's antics. He was so darn cute when he was happy and his belly was full. He was also extra adorable in the little choo-choo train overalls Alex had provided. He probably hadn't picked them out specifically, but whoever he'd put in charge of buying baby clothes had done an excellent job.

Raising a tightly closed fist into the air, Henry suddenly let out a squeal and jerked so hard, his seat scooted a good inch across the table. Jessica jumped, dropping the tiny Elmo spoon full of cereal and grabbing the seat before it could move any closer to the edge. Then she turned her head slightly to see what had gotten Henry so excited.

Alex stood only inches away, dressed in a charcoal suit and electric-blue tie that made his eyes pop like sapphires. He looked as though he'd just stepped off the pages of a men's fashion magazine. Or was maybe on the way to a photo shoot for one.

"Jeez, you scared me," she told him. Then she turned

back to Henry, picking up the fallen spoon and wiping up the spilled cereal with a damp cloth she had nearby.

When he didn't respond, and the awkward silence stretched from seconds into minutes, she craned her neck in his direction again. That's when she noticed the hard glint in his narrowed eyes and the still line of his mouth.

She swallowed and took a breath. "What's wrong?"

She'd never seen an expression like that on the face of anyone who wasn't there either to chew her out or tell her somebody had died. And with Alex she was betting on getting chewed out. What was it this time? she wondered.

"We need to talk," he told her simply, his voice sharp as a razor blade.

Uh-oh.

She looked back at Henry, her hand still on his carrier. His food-smeared smile was wide, his feet continuing to dance.

"Mrs. Sheppard," Alex intoned. "Can you please watch the baby while I have a word with Jessica?"

The housekeeper didn't seem thrilled with the prospect of babysitting duty, but dried her hands on a dish towel and crossed to the table, plucking the small plastic spoon from Jessica's fingers. Taking that as a sign that she didn't have much choice in the matter, Jessica relinquished the spoon and her seat, reluctantly following Alex from the kitchen.

Wordlessly, they walked to his office, where he waited for her to enter ahead of him, then shut the door behind them with a solid click of finality.

Much like the day before, she expected him to move behind his desk, and for both of them to sit down before he said whatever it was he had to say. Instead, he remained near the closed door, legs apart and arms crossing his chest in what could only be described as an aggressive stance.

"You're a Taylor," he blurted without preamble.

Her heart stuttered in her chest. "Excuse me?"

His eyes went to slits, a muscle ticking on one side of his jaw.

"Don't play dumb with me," he bit out. "Your name isn't Jessica Madison. It's Jessica Madison *Taylor*."

Eleven

The blood drained from Jessica's face. She felt it flush down her neck and through her body all the way to her toes, leaving her dizzy and light-headed.

Afraid she might actually faint, she took a step back, relieved when she bumped into one of the armchairs standing in front of his wide desk. She leaned her weight against it, reaching behind to dig her nails into the supple leather to help hold her upright and in place.

Licking her lips, she swallowed past the overwhelming drumbeat of her heart. Barely above a whisper, her voice grated out the only thought spiraling through her mind. "How did you find out?"

A flash of anger filled his expression. "DNA isn't the only thing I had tested. A friend on the police force ran your fingerprints for me, and they came back as Jessica Madison Taylor. No criminal record, I'm pleased to say, but it turns out you aren't at all who you claim to be. Your prints showed up as a former employee of both Mountain View and Bajoran Designs."

Well, not Bajoran Designs so much as Taylor Fine Jewels, when it existed. Still, she didn't know what to say. Shock that he'd found her out reverberated through every bone and nerve ending.

She certainly hadn't expected to be called out quite so soon. She'd actually been hoping she could find a time and place and way to tell him on her own. Eventually, when she couldn't keep it under wraps any longer.

"So what was your plan, exactly?" Alex asked, bitterness seeping into every syllable. "Seduce me for company secrets so you could sell them to the highest bidder? Or was the goal all along to get pregnant so you could blackmail me later with an heir?"

What little blood had worked its way back to her brain seeped out just as quickly. Her breath came in tiny, shallow gasps as her chest tightened and she swayed on her feet.

"What are you talking about?" she said, her jaw clenched. Partly because she was angry and partly because she was literally shaking. Her arms, her legs, her teeth. Every inch of her was quaking with the effort to hold back the maelstrom of emotions raging through her like a tidal wave. "I didn't get pregnant *on purpose*. And I didn't sell anything to anyone."

Alex didn't look as though he believed her.

"But I didn't get lucky with just a single, uninhibited chambermaid, did I? You're the daughter of Donald Taylor, granddaughter of *Henry* Taylor, both of whom used to be in partnership with Bajoran Designs. Aren't you?"

A beat passed before she answered. "Yes."

"And you just happened to be at the resort, cleaning *my* room."

She raised a brow, her grip on the chair at her back loosening as she began to regain some of her equilibrium.

"Actually, yes."

Doubt filled his stony features and was evident in his snort of derision.

"Call Mountain View. Give them my real name, and they'll tell you I was employed there long before you checked in. And the suite where you stayed was part of my regular rounds."

"Lucky for you that I landed there, then, wasn't it?"

"I wouldn't use the word *lucky,* no."

The day Alex had checked in to the resort was the beginning of her life's downward spiral. Except for Henry. He may have been unexpected, tossing her headfirst in a direction she wasn't ready to travel, but he was also the single greatest gift she'd ever been given.

"It was the perfect opportunity for you to take part in a bit of corporate espionage, though, hmm?"

Her pulse skipped in her veins. Wasn't that the exact term she'd used when Erin had first concocted her appalling plan? Of that, at least, she *was* guilty.

"I suppose you could say that, yes," she admitted. She wasn't proud of it, but the jig was obviously up, and she didn't intend to lie or deny any of it any longer.

"I recognized you the minute I saw you," she told him. "My family was devastated when you cut them off from Bajoran Designs and drove them out of business. I was okay with it, believe it or not. I might have ended up as merely a hotel maid, but I was happy and making enough of an income to live on. Unfortunately, the rest of my family didn't handle things quite as well."

Taking a deep breath, she released the rest of her hold on the armchair and moved on stiff legs to perch at the very edge of its overstuffed cushion. She was no longer facing Alex, cowering beneath his withering glare, but she didn't need to. His angry judgment filled the room like poison gas.

"When I mentioned to my cousin that you were staying at the resort, she convinced me to poke around your room. No excuses," she put in quickly, putting up a hand to hold off whatever his next verbal assault might be. "It was a stupid idea and I was wrong to ever agree to it, but I did. She wanted me to look for something that would hurt you—or rather, hurt Bajoran Designs. Something that could be used against you or put Taylor Fine Jewels back in operation."

"The design specs for the Princess Line," he said, his voice sharp as tacks.

Her head snapped up. So he knew she'd taken them. She'd kind of hoped she wouldn't have to confess that. But…

"Yes. I'm sorry about that."

"You seduced me to get them, and then sold the proposed designs to our competition."

The accusation struck her like a two-by-four. Her brows knit and she shook her head.

"No. No," she insisted. "I took them, but I didn't sell them. I never did anything with them."

"But you don't deny seducing me to get your hands on them," he tossed back with heavy sarcasm.

Spine straight, she lifted her chin and held his icy gaze. "Of course I do. I'm not a prostitute. I don't use my body to obtain information or anything else."

In for a penny, in for a pound, she thought before forging ahead. "I slept with you because I wanted to, and for no other reason. I'm also pretty sure *you* seduced me, not the other way around."

"I wouldn't be so certain of that," he muttered.

Stalking across the room, he rounded his desk and took a seat in front of the laptop set up there for his regular use. He tapped a few keys, waited a moment then turned the computer a hundred and eighty degrees so she could see the screen.

"Seduction aside, how do you explain this?" he asked.

She studied the images in front of her, growing colder by the second.

"I don't understand," she murmured.

Sliding forward, she looked even closer, narrowing her eyes, trying to figure out what was going on, how this had happened.

It had been months since she'd seen the original designs for the Princess Line, but she remembered them in acute detail. She'd even redesigned portions of them mentally and sketched changes in the margins of numerous pieces of paper that had passed through her hands since she'd taken them from his briefcase.

Nearly the *exact* designs from that folder were on the screen in front of her now, though, in rich, eye-popping color.

"What is this?" Swinging her gaze to Alex, she frowned. "Did Ignacio Jewelers buy the line concept from you? They needed work, but you shouldn't have given them up. They were perfect for Bajoran Designs."

His eyes turned to chips of blue glass, his fingers curling until the knuckles went white. "What kind of game are you playing, Jessica? I already know who you really are. I know what you were doing in my suite that night. You can stop with the lies."

"I'm not lying about anything," she said, growing more confused by the moment. "What are you talking about?"

"What are *you* talking about?" he demanded. "You know damn well you stole those designs from my briefcase that night after we slept together and sold them to Ignacio. I assume as part of your plot for revenge. Though why the hell you would have it in for me or my family's company, I'll never know."

Closing her eyes, Jessica shook her head and rubbed a spot near her temple where a headache was forming at record speed.

"No. This is…this is insane."

Opening her eyes again, she met his gaze head-on. "I told you I made a mistake in taking those designs. But I never did anything with them. I tried to return them the very next day, but you were already gone. Do you really think that if I'd sold them, I would be here now? That line of jewelry was worth millions. Even with a baby to care for, I couldn't have gone through that kind of money in under a year."

"I don't think you did," Alex told her. "I think you decided that showing up with a baby and telling me he's mine is all part of your plan to get even more money out of the Bajorans."

Tears prickled behind Jessica's lashes. "I'm sorry that I lied to you and betrayed your trust by taking those sketches," she said, struggling to keep her voice even and unwavering. "But no matter what you think of me, Henry *is* your son. I'm here because of him, *not* because I want anything from you. And I don't know what happened with that line," she rushed to add. "I don't know how Ignacio Jewelers got hold of it, but…I'll find out. Or at least I'll try."

Alex watched the myriad emotions playing over Jessica's delicate features. She looked truly distraught. Guilty and confused and hurt by his rapid-fire accusations.

It was no less than she deserved, of course, he thought to himself, clenching his jaw and refusing to be swayed by the moisture gathering in her eyes.

He wasn't sure what angered him most—the fact that she'd stolen the plans for one of his company's million-dollar ventures, or that she'd slept with him to get them.

That night might have been a one-night stand, but it sure as hell hadn't been meaningless. Not to him. Now he felt like a first class fool for ever thinking there was more between them than simply sex.

Crossing his arms in an attempt to rein in his temper, he arched a brow. "How, exactly, do you intend to do that?"

He could see the wheels in her head turning, desperately searching for a solution, a way out of the fix she was in.

Finally, she took a deep breath, her expression filling with resolve. "I left the proposal with the rest of my things when I stored them at my parents' house before leaving town. It should still be there."

"And who's to say you didn't simply make a copy before selling it out from under me?"

"I—" She screeched to a halt, blinking in confusion. "Why would I do that? I'd have no reason to keep a copy once I sold it for millions and millions of dollars to keep me in the wonderful lifestyle to which I've become so accustomed."

For having started out on a stammer, she ended with more than a fair note of snark. He had to bite the inside of his lip to keep from laughing aloud at her spunk.

Not for the first time, he was impressed by her resilience. She was in trouble, here. With his power and money, he could squash her like a bug if he so desired. Yet she was standing in front of him with her chin out and her "dare me" attitude wrapped around her like a shawl.

It also got him thinking. She was challenging him, and no one in their right mind would do that—not in this manner, about something so vital—unless they could back it up. Would they?

"So your assertion is that if the file is still there, hidden amongst your other belongings, then you couldn't have betrayed me and my family's company by selling it, is that it?"

"Yes."

"How do you intend to prove that?"

She took a deep breath, causing her breasts to rise beneath the lightweight material of her daffodil-yellow top. He wondered if it was one he'd had delivered for her, or if she'd brought it stuffed in that ridiculously small knapsack she'd been carrying when she'd arrived.

"I guess I'll have to go home and dig it out." A beat passed as she narrowed her gaze on him and pursed her lips. "Would you believe me if I did?"

Another challenge. Damned if he didn't like that about her. Not enough to give her a free pass, but the benefit of a doubt was a possibility.

"I'd consider it," he said carefully, not ready to promise anything he wouldn't later be willing to deliver.

"Well, that's encouraging," she mumbled half under her breath. Shaking her head, she straightened and looked him in the eye. "Tell me what you want me to do. Should I go to Portland and look for the file, or would you prefer to continue hating me for wrongs you *think* I committed?"

"Oh, you've committed plenty of wrongs, with or without the sale of that design line to our competitors," he reminded her even as he battled a grin.

She was guilty of so much, but she didn't let that hold her back one bit when it came to sticking up for herself. Arguing business with his contemporaries was definitely never this exhilarating.

Then again, no one at Bajoran Designs was as attractive or compelling as Jessica, and he'd never had quite as much to lose —or gain—if he suffered a defeat at their hands.

"We'll go together," he told her. "We can take the corporate jet. Be down there and back in a matter of hours."

Sucking her bottom lip between her teeth, she worried it for a moment, her face reflecting sudden alarm.

"What?" he asked. "Change your mind already? Decide to confess and put an end to the charade before we waste any more time or a load of jet fuel on a wild-goose chase?"

"You're an arrogant ass, do you know that?"

His brows rose. So much for the effectiveness of his harsh features and intimidating demeanor.

"If you must know," she continued sharply, "my parents don't know about Henry."

The shock must have shown in his expression because she flushed crimson and shifted guiltily in her chair.

"I know. I know how terrible that sounds," she admitted, tucking her hair behind one ear and running her fingertips through to the ends. "I'm a horrible daughter. It will crush them when they find out I've been lying and keeping a grandchild from them all this time."

"Then why did you?"

She cast him a glance meant to singe him on the spot. "Can you just hear that conversation? 'Hey, Mom and Dad, I know this will disappoint you, but I'm pregnant from a one-night stand. Oh, but that's not the best part. The *best* part is that the baby's father is our family's arch nemesis, Alexander Bajoran, the man who single-handedly ruined Taylor Fine Jewels and destroyed our lives. Surprise!'"

"Archenemy is a bit strong, don't you think?" he asked with an arched brow.

She gave a snort of derision. "Not amongst the Taylor clan. Your name might as well be Lucifer Bajoran, as far as they're concerned."

Which seemed to be an awfully harsh sentiment to have for a former business associate who hadn't had much at all to do with the split between their families. All of that had taken place quite literally before his time. Alex had been working at Bajoran Designs, of course, but hadn't taken over as CEO until well after the Taylors' departure.

He frowned to himself. Perhaps there was more to the story than he knew, more that he *should* know. He made a mental note to look into it when he got back to the Bajoran Designs offices. Out of curiosity, if nothing else.

"Then what do you propose?" he asked, focusing instead on the matter of visiting Portland so they could retrieve the Princess Line proposal. If it was even still where she claimed it was.

"If we go on Sunday, my parents will be at my aunt's house for brunch. They're usually gone three or four hours, so we should be able to get in and out before they get home."

He thought about that for a minute. "You're really going to sneak into town without letting your parents know you were there? After not seeing them in almost a year?"

Her chest shuddered as she took in a deep, unsteady breath. "If I have to, yes. I told you I was a terrible daughter," she added when he tipped his head quizzically. "I need to tell them, I know that. And I will. Soon. I just…I need time to work up to it, and frankly, I can only deal with one major crisis at a time. At the moment, *you* are the main crisis I'm dealing with."

"Then the sooner we get to the bottom of some very important facts, the better."

"Agreed."

"In that case, let me know exactly what time we need to be at your parents' house, and I'll make all of the arrangements for the trip, including someone to stay here with Henry."

He expected an argument over that, but all she did was nod. Apparently she, too, saw the wisdom in not dragging an infant along on a mission one step up from breaking and entering.

Twelve

"I don't understand. They were right here."

Jessica hoped her voice didn't reflect the panic beating in her chest and at her pulse points.

They were at her parents' home in Portland. A lovely two-story brick house at the end of cul-de-sac in a modest development.

The flight down had been uneventful, and only uncomfortable because Jessica didn't like being alone in such close quarters with Alex. If "alone" included a pilot in the cockpit and one very discreet flight attendant who made herself scarce between serving drinks and asking Mr. Bajoran if there was anything else he required. And if the private plane could be described as "close quarters." It wasn't as large as his mansion, but it wasn't exactly a broom closet, either.

She'd blamed her antsiness on a mild fear of flying and being away from Henry. Only one of those factors actually bothered her, but Alex didn't need to know that. And the sooner they found the folder and got back to Seattle, the better.

Back to her baby, who was probably even now being rocked to sleep by Wendy the nanny. She liked Wendy well enough; she was actually the nanny Jessica would have hired if it had been her choice alone. But that didn't mean she was keen on another woman caring for her child when she should be there with him instead.

The garage attached to her parents' home was large enough for two midsize cars—one of which was currently absent—and all of her belongings from when she'd had to clear out her apartment. Thankfully she didn't own much by way of material possessions.

Even so, she'd gone through everything. *Everything* because the folder with the Princess Line designs inside wasn't where she was almost positive she'd left it. She specifically remembered tucking it away with some of her other important papers and legal documents. Not only for safekeeping, but because she knew it would blend in and wasn't likely to be noticed if anyone snooped through her things.

She couldn't imagine her parents going through her stuff.

Her mother would be like a dog with a bone about the paternity of her first grandchild, but they weren't the nosy sort otherwise. For heaven's sake, she'd quit her job, given up her apartment and taken off for parts unknown, all on a whim, and they hadn't asked a single question. As far as they were concerned, she was traveling, sowing the female equivalent of wild oats and would call if she needed them. Otherwise they assumed no news was good news.

"Maybe they were never there to begin with, and this is just part of your elaborate ruse to convince me they were," Alex said from two or three feet behind her. He'd been standing there, hovering less than patiently while she searched.

"You'd like that, wouldn't you?" she retorted without turning around. She was still on her knees, digging through the same banker's box for the third time in thirty minutes. "One more nail to drive into my coffin. One more reason you'll give the courts to convince them I'm an unfit mother—a *criminal,* even—and that you deserve full custody of Henry."

Frustrated, angry and increasingly frightened he would do just that, she climbed to her feet, brushing off the knees of her jeans.

Facing him, she said, "Well, that isn't going to happen. I'm not lying, and this isn't a ruse. They were *there,* dammit, and I'm going to find out why they aren't anymore."

Big talk when she had no idea how to go about it. But she couldn't let Alex see her uncertainty, not when there was so much at stake.

Think. Think. Think.

Her erratic pulse suddenly slowed, and she realized she *wasn't* the only person who had known about the Princess Line proposal. She'd told her cousin. Shown her the designs, even.

Not to use them against Alex, but to prove she *had* poked around his room the way she'd promised, and also because she'd simply loved the designs. The artist in her had been impressed and unable to resist sharing them with someone she'd thought would appreciate their beauty and intricacy as much as she did. With a few notations on how she would improve upon them, if she could.

That's what they had discussed the morning she'd shown Erin the design sketches. *Not* how they could best go about selling them out from under Bajoran Designs. She would never have done that, regardless of what Alex might think.

As much as she wasn't looking forward to what she had to do, it needed to be done. She owed it to Alex, and at this point, to Henry and herself, too.

"Can I borrow your cell phone?" she asked.

Alex's eyes widened a fraction, the blue of the irises stormy and nearly gray. Whether due to mistrust or the dull light in the interior of the garage, she wasn't sure.

Without a word, he reached into the inside pocket of his suit jacket and removed his phone, handing it over.

Dialing by memory, she waited through three rings for her cousin to answer.

"Erin, it's Jessica." It was strange having this conversation in front of Alex, especially considering what she was about to say, but it wasn't as though she had much choice.

"Erin, this is important," she bit out, cutting into her cousin's fluffy, drawn-out greeting. Once Erin quieted, she said, "What did you do with the design folder I stole from Alexander Bajoran?"

Lord, it hurt to use that word—*stole*. But she'd taken it without permission, so she had to call it what it was.

"What do you mean?" her cousin asked. Too innocently. Even through the phone line, she could tell Erin was feigning naïveté.

"Don't play dumb with me, Erin. I mean it. This is important. I need you to tell me *right now* what you did with the Princess Line designs. I put them with my things in Mom and Dad's garage, but they're missing, and *you* are the only other person who even knew they existed."

Silence filled the space between them for several long seconds. Jessica didn't look at Alex. She couldn't. Instead, she pressed her fingers to the bridge of her nose and prayed she wouldn't break down in front of him, no matter how close to tears she felt.

Finally, in a tone of complete entitlement, her cousin said, "I sold them."

Jessica's heart sank. "Oh, Erin," she groaned, "tell me you didn't. *Please* tell me you didn't really do that."

"Of course I did," Erin replied without a hint of apology.

"That was the plan from the very beginning, after all. To stick it to those Bajoran bastards."

Despite her best efforts, tears leaked from Jessica's lashes. "No, it wasn't," she told her cousin, voice cracking. "That was never the plan. I *never* agreed to anything even close to that."

"Why else were you poking around the man's room, then?" Erin asked haughtily. As though she had any right to be offended.

"Because I was an idiot," Jessica snapped. "And because you convinced me I needed to do something to avenge the family against the evil Bajorans. Which is the most ridiculous idea in history and the stupidest thing I've ever done."

Taking a deep, shuddering breath, she dropped her hand from her face and turned away from Alex. She couldn't bear to look at him or have him look at her, at least directly, while she was making such a soul-shattering confession.

"You had no right to go through my things, Erin. No more right to take that proposal from me than I had to take it from Alex." Her voice was ragged, and she was skating close to the very edge of hysteria. "You have no idea what you've done, Erin."

"Oh, what did I do?" her cousin retorted, snottier than Jessica had ever heard her. "Get a little revenge against a corporate tycoon who used his money and influence to put our family out of business? Make some well-deserved money of my own while screwing the Bajorans out of another couple million they *didn't* deserve? So what."

"No," Jessica murmured, forcing herself to speak past the lump in her throat. "What you've done is betray my trust. Worse, you've done irreparable damage to my life. My reputation. My *son's* life. I can't forgive you for this, Erin. Not ever."

She clicked the button to end the call just as her voice

broke and her lungs started to fight against her efforts to draw in fresh oxygen.

How could Erin have done this to her? She'd convinced Jessica to do the wrong thing, true. And Jessica took full responsibility for having actually done the snooping and taking of the papers.

But she hadn't truly planned to do anything with them. Had fully intended to put them back, and suffered months of guilt when she hadn't been able to. She'd almost traveled all the way to Seattle to return them in person, but had been too afraid Alex would call the police and have her arrested.

That, in fact, had been one of her greatest fears about returning to Seattle with Henry. She'd been beyond lucky that he'd put their son first and not called the authorities on her the moment she stepped into his house.

"Are you all right?"

He spoke softly, his tone kinder than she would have expected given the circumstances. In fact, he hadn't sounded quite so nice since that night at the resort when he'd been intent on getting her into bed. Or according to him, open to allowing her to seduce him.

His hand touched her shoulder. Lightly, almost comfortingly.

Fresh moisture glazed her vision. How could he be so understanding *now* when the evidence was clearly stacked against her? He should be furious. Sharp and accusing, just like before.

"Jessica?" he prompted again.

She shook her head. "I am definitely not all right," she told him with a watery laugh.

Turning back to the stacks and boxes of her things, she started replacing lids and putting everything back in order. It was busywork, something to keep her hands occupied so she wouldn't sit down right in the middle of the hard concrete garage floor and sob uncontrollably.

"I guess that's it," she threw over her shoulder in Alex's general direction. "You win. Erin took the proposal and sold the designs to Ignacio, just like you thought I had. So there's no way to prove my innocence. No way to convince you I'm not the lying, thieving bitch you accused me of being."

"I don't remember using the term *bitch*."

Sliding the last cardboard box onto a short pile of other boxes, she turned to face him. Calmer now, more composed. Resigned.

"I'm pretty sure it was implied," she said, emotionless now.

"No, but perhaps it was inferred," he replied.

Moving toward her, he stopped mere inches away. She still couldn't bring herself to meet his eyes, so she stared at a spot on his blue-and-black-striped tie instead.

"I should probably apologize for that," he continued, surprising her enough that she lifted her head. "I might have been a bit more critical of your actions than was warranted."

Jessica's mouth didn't actually fall open in a big wide O, but she was certainly shocked enough that it should have.

He was apologizing? To her? But she didn't deserve it. She may not have been guilty of *exactly* what he'd accused her of, but she'd undoubtedly put it all in motion.

She hadn't set out to seduce him or to get pregnant, but both had happened because she'd been poking her nose where it didn't belong.

And she hadn't sold the designs for the Princess Line to a competing company, but she had taken them and shown them to her cousin, who'd done just that.

Cocking her head, she studied him through narrowed eyes. "Did I accidentally drop one of those boxes on your head?"

she asked him. And then, "Who are you and what have you done with Alexander Bajoran?"

She was too upset and emotionally wrung dry to mean it as a joke, but one corner of his mouth lifted nonetheless.

"I heard both sides of the conversation. Enough to get the general idea, anyway, and to accept that it was, indeed, your cousin who sold the line proposal to Ignacio Jewelers. Which isn't to say you don't still carry some of the responsibility," he added with a note of severity he wasn't sure he felt.

"What are you saying?" Jessica asked, justifiably suspicious. "That you just…forgive me? Absolve me of guilt for everything I've done since we first met?"

"I wouldn't go quite that far," he replied dryly. "But I'd be a hypocrite—as well as a heel—if I held you responsible for something you didn't technically do. I'll talk to our attorneys, see if there's anything we can do about your cousin's spin at corporate espionage."

He paused to gauge her reaction to that, expecting anything from a heated defense of her family member to hysterical tears and begging for leniency. Instead, her full lips pulled into a taut line and her shoulders went back a fraction.

"I'm sorry," he said, "but we have to at least look into it. Losing those plans cost us millions of dollars."

"No, of course," she responded quickly. "What Erin did was wrong. What *I* did was wrong, but I never would have taken it as far as she did. She made her bed…I guess she'll have to lie in it."

"Strange as it might sound," Alex told her, "I actually believe you."

And he did. Not only because of what he'd heard with his own two ears, but because if she'd made a dime off the Princess Line prospectus, she would have shown at least a modicum of guilt. Or been dancing like a spider on a hot plate trying to wiggle her way out of trouble.

He even had to wonder about his assertion that she'd seduced him that night back at Mountain View to get her hands on company secrets. If that were true, she wouldn't have wasted a moment now trying to seduce him into letting her transgressions slide.

But she wasn't fast-talking, and she didn't have her hand down his pants. More's the pity on the latter. She'd simply admitted her part in the whole ordeal, all but assuming the position and waiting for the cops to slap on cuffs.

That was not the behavior of a liar, a cheat or—quite frankly—a gold digger. The verdict was still out on Henry and her purpose in leaving the baby in his boardroom. But since she'd been telling the truth about the majority of charges he'd leveled against her…well, there was a fair chance she was telling the truth about the rest.

Clearing his throat, he stuffed his hands in the front pockets of his slacks to keep from doing something stupid like reaching out to touch her. And not to console her.

He wanted to brush the lock of loose blond hair dusting her cheek back behind her ear. Maybe slide his hand the rest of the way to her nape, thread his fingers into the soft curls there, tug her an inch or two closer….

And from there his thoughts took a decidedly hazardous turn. Better to keep his hands to himself before he risked complicating matters even more than they were already.

"Just because I believe you about your cousin doesn't mean you're off the hook," he told her in a voice that came out rougher than he would have liked.

That roughness wasn't caused by anger but by the fact that he was suddenly noticing the bounce of her blond curls—sans the blue streak of a year ago. The alabaster smoothness of her pale skin. The rosy swell of her lush, feminine lips. And the slight dusting of gray beneath the hazel brown of her eyes, attesting to the stress she'd been under for…he suspected months now.

He hadn't exactly helped alleviate that stress, either, had he? No, he'd added to it in every possible way from the moment she'd walked into his home.

With good reason, he'd thought at the time. But not such good reason now that he knew she wasn't quite the conniving witch he'd made her out to be.

"At the very least," he intoned, "I'd say you owe me one."

She stared at him with eyes gone dull with wariness. "Owe you one…what?"

Rather than answer that question directly, he shrugged a shoulder and finally reached out to take her hand. "I've got something in mind. In the meantime I think we should get out of here. The jet is waiting, and your parents will probably be back soon."

With more familiarity than he thought she realized she was showing, she grabbed his wrist and turned it to glance at the face of his watch.

"You're right, we should go."

She didn't look any happier about leaving than she had when they'd arrived.

"I'm sorry we didn't find what we came here for," she muttered softly as they headed for the garage's service door.

"That's okay." He let her pass first, then followed, closing and locking the door behind them. "I know just how you'll make it up to me."

Thirteen

Though she asked a handful of times on the flight home exactly how Alex expected her to "make it up to him," he wouldn't give her so much as a hint of his plans. Rather than put her out of her misery, he merely smiled a cruel and wicked smile and let her squirm.

Hmph. He was probably enjoying her suffering. He probably didn't have a single clue yet what he was going to ask of her as so-called "repayment"—he just liked having her dangle like a little worm at the end of his hook.

And there was nothing she could do about it. She was at his mercy.

Hunched in the plush leather window seat, the sound of engines roaring in the background, she tried to hold on to her indignation and put on a full pout. The only problem was, she'd never been much of the pouting type. She also knew she deserved a bit of payback for what she'd done to Alex, both the intentional and the unintentional.

That didn't mean she was going to let him walk all over her. If he said he wanted her to assassinate the president or be his sex slave for a month, she'd know he was a crazy person and wasn't as interested in compensation as simply using and abusing her. But if he just wanted her to eat a little crow, she would do her best to sprinkle it with seasoning and choke it down.

Twenty minutes later the plane landed, and Alex accompanied her onto the tarmac and straight to the shiny black Lexus waiting for them. A private airstrip employee opened the passenger-side door, waiting for her to slide inside before rounding the hood and handing the keys to Alex.

They rode in silence until Jessica realized they weren't headed for Alex's estate. At first she thought she just wasn't familiar enough with the area. And then that he was taking a shortcut...except that it turned out to be a long cut. She remembered the route they'd taken from the house to the airport, and this wasn't the reverse of that.

"Where are we going?" she finally asked, finding her voice for the first time in more than an hour.

"You'll see," was all he said, strong fingers wrapped around the steering wheel.

She didn't sigh, at least not aloud. But she did sit up straighter, fiddling with the safety strap crossing her chest while she studied each of the street signs and storefronts as they passed.

Before long, he slowed, easing effortlessly into a parking space in front of a shop called Hot Couture. Sliding out of the car, he came around, opened her door and pulled her up by the hand.

She began to ask again where they were going, but bit down on her tongue before she started to sound like a broken record. He led her across the wide sidewalk and inside the upscale boutique.

Okay, she had to say something. "What are we doing here?"

Everywhere she looked, headless size-zero mannequins were draped in costly bolts of silk, satin, sequins and a dozen other expensive materials she couldn't begin to identify. She'd been away from this sort of extravagance for too long...and hadn't cared for it all that much when she'd been expected to wear gowns like these on a regular basis.

"This is Step One of your penance," he told her as they were approached by a saleswoman who looked as though she'd had her facial features lifted one too many times. Her eyes were a tad too wide, her brows a tad too high, her lips a tad too pursed.

"Good afternoon," she greeted them, focusing her attention much more firmly on Alex than on Jessica. With good reason—Alex looked like every one of the million-plus dollars he was worth, while Jessica was dressed in a pair of worn jeans and a stylish but nondesigner top. They were Daddy Warbucks and Little Orphan Annie...Richard Gere and Julia Roberts...the Prince and the Pauperette.

She rubbed her palms nervously on the legs of her jeans. "This isn't necessary, Alex," she murmured so that only he could hear.

At full volume, he replied, "Yes, it is." Then to the other woman, "We need a gown for a very important gala fundraiser. Shoes and handbag, as well."

The woman looked positively giddy at the prospect of a large commission.

"Alex..." Jessica began.

"I'll take care of the jewelry," he said over the beginning of her protests.

"What kind of fundraiser?" she asked, wanting to know at least that much before she began trying on a year's worth of dresses in the next couple of hours.

"Sparkling Diamonds," he said, naming the well-known charitable organization founded and run by Washington State's most notable jewelers. Since its inception only a few years ago, Sparkling Diamonds had raised hundreds of thousands of dollars to support a variety of worthwhile causes, from childhood cancer to local animal shelters.

"Tuesday night's benefit is being sponsored solely by Bajoran Designs. Some of Seattle's deepest pockets will be there, and we want to rake in as much as possible for this year's literacy campaign. I was planning to go stag, but now that you're here and—as we established—owe me one," he tacked on with an uncharacteristic wink, "you can be my plus-one."

Jessica wasn't entirely sure how she felt about that. Getting dressed up and going to a swanky party with Alex? Hanging on his arm all night with a smile on her face while they mingled with people who might recognize her as a Taylor Fine Jewels Taylor? Oh, the rumor mills would be rife with chatter after that. Word might even get back to her parents.

She thought she might prefer to undergo an extra hot bikini wax. But then, she didn't have much of a choice, did she? And after her conversation with Erin, the cat was pretty much out of the bag, anyway.

"Literacy is important," she said by way of answer.

"Yes," he agreed, rare amusement glittering in his too-blue eyes, "it is. The event is also a chance to show off a few of the company's latest designs. Ones we've been unveiling instead of the Princess Line."

There it was. Knife inserted and twisted forty degrees clockwise. It pinched, just as he'd known it would.

"You'll be wearing the most significant pieces. Yellow gold and diamonds, so they'll go with almost anything."

Turning his attention back to the saleslady, he said, "I want her to look absolutely stunning. Find a dress that showcases her natural beauty."

Inside her chest, Jessica's heart fluttered, heat unfurling just below the surface of her skin. If she weren't fully aware of the situation and where each of them stood, it would be all too easy to be flattered by that comment. After all, Alex was a very charming man. Isn't that how she'd ended up in bed with him in the first place?

But he wasn't trying to be charming. He wanted her dressed up and pretty to impress donors at his charity event. She was sorely out of practice, but that was something she could definitely do.

"Yes, sir," the woman replied, money signs glowing in her eyes along with her wide smile.

Jessica followed her silently to the rear of the store, listening with only half an ear to the older woman's cheerful chatter. Leaving Jessica in the changing room to strip, she went in search of gowns that would meet Alex's high standards.

An hour later, Jessica felt like a quick-change artist. She was tired and out of sorts, and just wanted to get home to see Henry.

She'd tried on so many dresses, she couldn't remember them all. After viewing the first few, even Alex had seemed to lose interest. He'd made low, noncommittal noises, then told her he trusted her to make a final decision before wandering off to talk on his cell phone.

Another six or eight gowns later, Jessica was pretty sure she'd found one that would pass muster. It was hard to be sure how anything would look with the jewelry he had in mind, since she hadn't actually seen the pieces for herself, but he'd described them briefly and she did her best to imagine them with each of the gowns she modeled.

She needed just the right color, just the right neckline. Just enough sparkle to shine, but not *out*shine the jewelry itself.

She'd forgotten how stressful the whole socialite thing could be. There was a reason she hadn't missed it. Much.

It didn't help, either, that her performance needed to be perfect this time. It wasn't just a public appearance or a high-priced fundraiser. It was one of her only options for redemption with Alex and getting into his good graces. There was still so much he could hold against her. So many ways he could punish her, if he so desired.

Licking her dry lips, she finished putting on her street clothes, then carried the gown she'd decided on—albeit uncertainly—out of the dressing room.

"We'll take this one," she told the sales lady.

"Excellent choice," the woman agreed, taking the gown and carrying it to the counter.

Jessica was pretty sure she'd have said the same thing about a gunny sack, as long as Alex was willing to pay a high four figures for it.

A few minutes, later she had shoes and a matching clutch, all of it wrapped up with tissue paper in pretty boutique boxes, ready to go. When the sales woman recited the total, Jessica's eyes just about bugged out of her head and her throat started to close.

It was almost as though she was having an allergic reaction to spending so much money for *one* night out on the town. She had half a notion to tell Alex that if everybody who planned to attend the fundraiser would simply donate the amount they would have spent on getting dressed up for the evening, they wouldn't need to hold the event at all.

It had been a long time since she'd poured money like that into anything that couldn't be eaten, driven or lived in, but the outrageous total wouldn't make a man like Alex so much as blink.

As though to prove her point, he seemed to appear out

of nowhere, passing his platinum card to the clerk over her shoulder.

The sales woman flashed a delighted grin. Thirty seconds later, Alex and Jessica were headed back to the car, expensive packages in tow.

"You found something you like, I take it?" he said once they were on the road again, finally on their way to his estate.

A knot of eager anticipation tightened in her stomach. She couldn't wait to get there and see her baby. They'd only been gone a day—not even a full day, really—but she wasn't used to being away from him. She'd missed him and wanted to see how he'd fared with the nanny Alex had hired—possibly on a permanent basis.

"Yes," she responded, trying to keep her mind focused on the conversation rather than the fact that Alex was driving the speed limit. He could have gone a *few* miles over without risking a ticket, for heaven's sake.

"I hope it's all right. It was hard to pick something to go with the jewelry you have in mind when I couldn't actually try them on together."

"I'm sure they'll be fine. The fundraiser starts at eight. Dinner will be served around nine-fifteen. Can you be ready to leave by seven?"

"Of course." It wasn't as though she had anything else to do or anywhere else to be aside from wandering around Alex's enormous house and spending time with Henry. She could be ready by seven o'clock *tonight,* if he needed her to be.

And in a way, she wished they were attending the charity function tonight. At least then it would be over and she wouldn't have to spend the next day and a half dreading the evening to come.

Alex stood in his den, one hand braced against the mantle of the carved marble fireplace, the other slowly swirling the ice cubes in his glass of scotch. He studied the empty hearth, lost in thought.

Jessica would be down soon to leave for the Sparkling Diamonds fundraiser. How the evening would proceed wasn't at the forefront of his mind, but Jessica certainly was.

After discovering that she wasn't the mastermind behind the theft of the Princess Line designs, he'd begun to wonder what else he might have been wrong about where she was concerned. Could she be telling the truth about everything?

She wasn't one hundred percent innocent, that was for sure. But for each wrongdoing he knew about or had accused her of, she'd come clean.

So what if she was also telling the truth about Henry being his son? He hoped she was, actually. It was a can of worms just waiting to be opened, but having Jessica and the baby under his roof had turned out to be a unique and surprisingly enjoyable experience.

He was just as attracted to Jessica now as he had been the first time he saw her. No matter what had happened in the year since, he still wanted her. His mouth still went dry the minute she walked into the room. His fingers still itched to stroke her skin and peel the clothes off her warm, pliant body.

And the baby...well, he'd been more than a little put off at first, but now he had to admit he was quite smitten. It was hard as hell to wear a mask of indifference, waiting to find out *for sure* whether or not Henry was his son. Not when he spent every day wanting to shed his suit and get down on the floor to tickle the baby's belly, dangle brightly colored plastic keys or play hide-and-seek behind his own hands just to hear the little boy giggle.

Then at night he lay in his big king-size bed imagining Jessica down the hall, sleeping alone. More than once he'd nearly tossed back the covers and marched over to join her...

or drag her back to sleep with him. Not that he had any intention of letting her fall asleep.

Pushing away from the fireplace, he crossed to his desk, setting aside his drink to flip open the file he'd read once before. He needed time to digest the information inside, figure out exactly what to do about it. But even as he rolled it over in his head, he looked the papers over again and was just as stunned and sickened as he'd been when he'd first seen them.

Jessica had mentioned that her cousin blamed him for the Taylors being driven out of business with Bajoran Designs. To his knowledge the decision had been mutually arrived at by the individual heads of each company. At the time that had been Jessica's father as CEO and her uncle—Erin's father, as it turned out—as CFO on the Taylor Fine Jewels side, and Alex's father as CEO and Alex's uncle as CFO on the Bajoran Designs side.

Both companies had been started separately by brothers—Alex's and Jessica's grandfathers and great-uncles. Then they'd joined together because all four brothers had met, formed a strong bond of friendship and thought Fate was trying to tell them something. And it had been a wonderful, very lucrative partnership for many years.

As far as Alex knew, the Taylors had simply decided to go back to being a separate business. His father had assured him the split was amicable and that everything had been taken care of before he'd retired and Alex had taken his place.

Of course what Alex and his family had learned only *after* his father had stepped down, and a few months before his death, was that the elder Bajoran's memory had started to slip. From the moment Alex had taken over the role of CEO, he'd been putting out small fires that his father had unintentionally set ablaze.

This, though…this wasn't a small fire, it was a damn inferno.

Oh, nothing that would harm Bajoran Designs. On the contrary, Bajoran Designs had come out miles upon miles above Taylor Fine Jewels.

But that made Alex far from happy. The bottom line was not more important to him than honor, integrity and proper business ethics. He didn't feel good about the fact that they'd apparently forced the Taylors out of the partnership and probably screwed them out of millions in profits.

The question now became *who* was responsible for that turn of events. It wasn't his father. The man might not be here to defend himself or even question, but Alex knew in his bones that his father would never have done something like that. Not to a business partner, and especially not to one he also considered a friend.

He highly doubted it had been his uncle, either. The two brothers were cut from the same cloth—honest and trustworthy to a fault.

The company investigators he'd put on the case had turned up these initial records fairly quickly, but they hadn't yet tracked down the name of the person who had put this ball in motion. He expected the information to come through any day now, and then he would have to deal with it.

But that was business. Jessica was personal, and he wasn't quite sure what to do about her or the way this information impacted her, as well as the rest of her family.

At the very least an apology was in order, even though he'd awakened that morning thinking she still owed him one.

A soft tap at his office door had him straightening up, closing the file and slipping it into one of the desk drawers for safekeeping. Then, clearing his throat, he called, "Come in."

Mrs. Sheppard poked her head in and said, "Miss Taylor asked me to tell you she's ready and waiting in the foyer."

"Thank you."

The nanny—who was turning out to be an excellent

choice, despite Jessica's original protests—was already upstairs with Henry, and his driver had been sitting outside in
the limo for the past half hour. Grabbing the jewelry box he'd
brought home with him that afternoon and the lightweight
camel hair coat he'd had special ordered for Jessica for this
evening, he headed toward the front of the house, his footsteps echoing in the cavernous emptiness.

He saw just the back of her head over one of the main
stairwell's newel posts as he rounded the corner. Then, as
he drew closer, she heard his approach, turned and took a
step in his direction.

His heart lurched, slamming against his rib cage hard
enough to bruise, and he faltered slightly, nearly tripping
over his own two feet.

This was why he'd had to walk away at the boutique on
Sunday. He'd waited while she'd changed into two different
gowns, then stepped out of the dressing room looking like a
supermodel hitting the end of a Paris runway...or an angel
dropped straight from Heaven.

His heart had thudded then, too, threatening to burst right
out of his chest, and other parts of his body had jumped to
attention. Whether it was a white spaghetti strap sheath or
long-sleeved red number, she'd made everything she put on
look like a million bucks.

He'd had to feign indifference and use phone calls as an
excuse to escape before he'd done something phenomenally
stupid, like giving the saleslady a hundred dollars to take off
and lock the door behind her so he could push Jessica into
the changing room and make love to her right up against the
wall. He'd broken into a cold sweat just thinking about it.

And that was before she'd landed on *the* dress, added ac-
cessories and done her hair and makeup to match. She was
so beautiful, she literally took his breath away. His lungs
burned from a lack of oxygen, but he couldn't have cared less.

The dress she'd chosen was a sapphire-blue that leaned toward turquoise and made the hazel of her eyes positively pop. It would have clashed horribly with the rebellious near-navy blue stripe that used to be in her hair. Her now all-blond tresses were swept up from her nape, held in place by invisible pins to leave her shoulders and the column of her long neck bare.

The gown was classically understated. A strapless, slightly curved bodice hugging the swell of her breasts…a wide swath of sparkling rhinestones circling the high waist…and yards of flowing blue fabric falling to the floor, with a sexy slit running all the way up to reveal a mouthwatering expanse of long, sleek leg when she moved.

Though she'd balked, Alex had finally convinced her to go into town for a quick mani-pedi. The pampering had done her good, and he'd been sure to spin the suggestion as part of the payback for her lies and thievery. And now her freshly painted toes peeked out of the strappy, diamond-studded heels that poked out from beneath the hem of the gown.

Alex didn't know how long he'd been standing there, drooling like a dog over a particularly juicy steak, but it must have been a while because Jessica's eyes narrowed in concern and she glanced down the line of her own body, checking for flaws. Of which there were absolutely none.

"What's wrong?" she asked, returning her gaze to his. "Don't you like the dress? I told you I shouldn't be the one to choose. It's *your* fundraiser, you should have—"

He cut her off midrant. "The dress is fine. More than fine," he said, grateful his voice came out only a shade rusty and choked.

Her chest rose as she inhaled a relieved breath, drawing his attention to all that lovely pale skin and the shadow of her cleavage. He couldn't decide if he was delighted or annoyed that he now got to decorate it with some of the shining jewels from Bajoran Designs' most recent unveiling.

He knew they would look amazing on her, even if she outshone them just a bit. But on the downside, draping her neck with shimmering diamonds would drag everyone else's eye to something he preferred to keep to himself.

"Do you have the jewelry you want me to wear?" she asked, seeming to read his mind.

He held out the large leather case, embossed in gold with the Bajoran Designs logo. Flipping open the lid, he let her see what lay on the blanket of black velvet inside.

"Oh," she breathed, reaching out red-tipped fingers to touch the necklace's center gem. "They're beautiful."

And yet they paled in comparison to the woman standing in front of him.

Tossing the coat he'd gotten for her over the banister, he set the jewelry box on the flat top of the newel. "Here, let me put them on you."

He started with the bracelet, slipping it on her wrist, and then the oversize dinner ring on the middle finger of her opposite hand. Her ears, normally glittering with multiple studs and tiny hoops, were completely bare, leaving room for his earrings and his earrings alone. Since he didn't want to hurt her, poking around trying to get the fish hooks into the proper holes, he handed the three-inch dangle earrings to her and let her insert them on her own.

"Spin around," he told her, reaching for the pièce de résistance.

Lifting the necklace up and over her head, he waited for her to arrange it in just the right spot before fastening the latch at the back of her neck. He let his fingers linger on her smooth skin, lightly stroking the tendons that ran from nape to shoulders, down to the delicate jut of her collarbones and then back up to cup her shoulders, stroking all the way down the length of her arms.

Circling one wrist, he lightly tugged her around to face him once again. The diamonds at her throat and ears twinkled in the light of the giant chandelier far overhead. But his gaze wasn't locked on the priceless set of jewels that were supposed to be the focal point of tonight's event. Instead, he was struck mute by the brilliant facets of Jessica herself.

Her fingers fluttered up to touch the netted V-shape of the necklace crossing her chest. Even without seeing them ahead of time, she'd chosen the most ideal gown possible to display the jewelry he'd intended to have her wear.

"Would you be offended if I said this set is much prettier than most of the pieces in the Princess Line?" she asked.

He gave a low chuckle. Leave it to Jessica to speak her mind, even when she thought she was in the doghouse.

"It better be. We really had to scramble to make up for that loss. We needed something to release in its place that would make just as much of a splash. Or so we hoped."

She tugged one corner of her lower lip, glossy with red lipstick, between her teeth. "Are you trying to make me feel worse about that than I already do?"

"Actually, no. I wouldn't give up this moment, seeing you in this dress wearing these particular pieces, for anything in the world."

She blinked at him, eyes round with disbelief. He was a little surprised that the words had come from his own mouth, but he wasn't sorry. After all, it was the absolute truth.

Another absolute truth was that if he'd had a choice in the matter, he'd say to hell with the Sparkling Diamonds fundraiser, scoop Jessica into his arms and carry her upstairs to his bed where she belonged. Or where he wanted her, at any rate. Almost more than his next breath.

His hand tightened on her wrist and he had to make a concerted effort to lighten his grip before he hurt her. Or followed through on his baser instincts.

"We should go," he murmured reluctantly. Lifting his free hand, he brushed the back of his knuckles along her cheek to her ear, pretending to straighten an earring.

She gave a small nod, but didn't look any more eager to move than he was.

"Here," he said, reaching for the ladies' camel hair coat. He was glad now that he'd chosen to order one in black. It went beautifully with her gown, but would have gone with a dress of any other color, as well.

He held it for her and she turned to slip her arms into the sleeves. Pulling the front closed, she lightly knotted the belt at her waist then took his elbow when he offered.

Crossing the polished parquet floor and stepping outside to climb into the waiting limousine, Alex let himself imagine, just for a moment, that this was real. That Jessica was his and that going out with her for a night on the town was the most normal thing in the world.

As would be coming home late, crawling into the same bed together and making love until dawn.

Fourteen

Two hours into the fundraiser, Jessica was ready to go home. Not because it wasn't enjoyable, but simply because she'd forgotten how exhausting events like this could be.

Once the thousand-dollar-a-plate dinner had been served and consumed, it was all about mingling. Rubbing elbows, making polite conversation, promoting your company and raising money for the cause du jour.

To his credit, Alex was a pro at it. There must have been close to two hundred people in attendance, but he acted as though each person he talked to was the *only* person in the room. He was charming and handsome, and positively oozed self-confidence.

Everyone they met was treated to the same suave greeting, which included introductions, questions about the other person's family and/or business, and then idle chitchat until Alex found an opening to bring up both a reference to Bajoran Designs and a request for a healthy donation. Jessica didn't know who was in charge of collecting checks, but she would be willing to bet his or her head was spinning in delight by now.

She was also relieved that even though Alex was introducing her by her real name, and she was sure most of the guests recognized her for exactly who she was, nobody seemed to be giving her curious looks or talking behind their hands about a Taylor returning to the fold on the arm of a Bajoran.

That wasn't to say the grapevine wouldn't be ripe with fresh rumors by morning, but at least no one was making an issue of it this evening.

Breaking away from the latest group of smiling faces, Alex put a hand at the small of her back and led her on their continued circuit of the room.

In addition to key Bajoran Designs executives and board members wearing the latest pieces of jewelry to show off, there were blown-up full-color signboards on easels arranged throughout the large ballroom featuring other Bajoran designs. It was an enticing display. Jessica had noticed more than one woman already decked out in her weight's worth of gold and jewels admiring what Jessica suspected would be her—or more likely, her husband's—next acquisition.

And for some reason she was inordinately pleased. She loved the jewelry business, loved the sparkle of priceless gems and the intricacies of the designs themselves. Hadn't realized just how much she'd missed it, actually. And even though she and her family were no longer involved in it the way they'd once been, she still wanted Alex's company to be successful.

Alex slowed his step when he noticed her studying one of the extraneous designs more closely than the others photographed on a background of bright pink satin.

"Do you like it?" he asked softly.

"Of course. Your company does very nice work."

"Very nice?" he replied.

When she tipped her head in his direction, she saw that one dark brow was notched higher than the other.

"Shouldn't you be swooning and dreaming of the day you can wear that necklace around your own neck?"

She gave a low chuckle. She was already wearing a lovely necklace from Bajoran Designs worth probably twice as much as the one in the oversize photo. Not that either of them would be very practical in her day-to-day life unless she sold them for things like food and diapers.

To Alex she said, "You forget that I used to be around jewelry like this all the time. After a while it loses a bit of its allure."

He leaned down to whisper in her ear. "Shh. Don't let anyone hear you say that or we'll lose customers."

She laughed again. "Sorry," she returned in an equally low, equally conspiratorial voice.

"So why were you studying this one so intently?"

Shrugging a bare shoulder, she turned back to it. "There are just a few things I would have done differently, that's all."

It took a second for Alex to reply. Then he asked, "Like what?"

She worried her bottom lip for a moment, not sure she should say anything. Then with a sigh, she decided she probably couldn't get into any more trouble with him than she already was.

"The metalwork is a bit heavy-handed," she said, pointing to the spots she was talking about. "These stones don't need that thick a setting. If the gold were a bit thinner, more of the emeralds would show and the whole thing would have more sparkle to it."

One beat passed, then two.

"What else?" he asked.

"I might have gone with more slope to the design." She ran

her finger over the outline of the piece to illustrate her point. "This is very boxy, whereas more curvature would lay better against a woman's chest and be more appealing to the eye."

This time, more than a couple of beats passed in silence. She'd counted well past ten and begun to sweat before she twisted slightly to face him.

His expression was inscrutable. The only thing she could tell was that his eyes had gone dark and he was studying her as though he expected her to burst into flames at any moment. And she just might, if her embarrassment grew much hotter.

She opened her mouth to apologize, backpedal as much as possible, but he cut her off.

"How do you know so much about this stuff?"

Caught off guard, she rolled her eyes and said the first thing that popped into her head. "Hello? Jessica Taylor, Taylor Fine Jewels. I told you, I grew up around all of this. Before my family and your family went their separate ways, I was in line to start designing for the company on an official basis. But even before then, my father let me offer suggestions on existing design specs."

She turned toward the crowd, watching until she spotted just the right example. "See that woman standing over there in the too-short red dress?"

Alex followed her line of sight. "I don't think it's too short."

With a snort, Jessica murmured to herself, "Of course you don't." He probably didn't think the dress was too tight for the woman's build, either, considering how much of her breasts were popping out.

Then to him she said, "The earrings and necklace she's wearing are mine. Marquise-cut diamonds in a white gold setting, with a lone ruby as the main focal point. My father made me work with one of the company's design teams, but only to be sure everything was done correctly. Otherwise, he told them to give me free reign."

Jessica could feel that she was smiling from ear to ear, but she couldn't help it. Perfecting and designing those pieces, working at her family's company and having her father show so much faith in her had been one of the happiest times of her life. She'd so been looking forward to doing that every day. Not just on a whim or trial basis, but as a career.

For the first time, she realized she shouldn't have given up on that dream so easily. She'd been so busy starting a new life that she'd lost sight of those goals. Even if it had been in another city, for another company, she should have found a way to continue designing.

Once again the stretch of silence from Alex brought her head around. His sharp blue gaze made her pulse skitter and sent a shiver rippling under her skin.

"The only other time I've ever seen you smile like that is when you're playing with Henry," he told her, his tone so low and intense, her chest grew too tight for her lungs to draw in a breath. "Why didn't I know about any of this before?"

Jessica blinked, her fingers curling into the palm of one hand and around the rhinestone-studded satin clutch in the other. He was moving too fast for her, jumping from business to personal, personal to business, too quickly for her to keep up. Not with the conversation, but with the feelings he was stirring inside of her and with what she *thought* he might be conveying with his suddenly severe expression.

Was the heat of his gaze banked passion or tightly controlled anger? She couldn't tell for sure, but from the arousal coiling low in her belly, she found herself hoping it was the former. As dangerous as that thought was.

Licking her dry lips and swallowing until she thought she could manage clear and normal speech, she said, "I guess my father never told anyone. Maybe he was waiting to see how I performed and whether my pieces actually sold before taking steps to hire me into the company officially."

Reaching out, he brushed a tendril of hair away from her face, letting the backs of his fingers skim her cheek. Sparks of electricity went off in her bloodstream at the contact, raising goose bumps over every inch of her flesh.

"We didn't manufacture very many of that design," he said softly, the words barely penetrating her hormone-addled brain. "But they sold very, very well."

She blinked, pleasure flooding her at his admission.

"I even remember commenting that we needed to put out more pieces like that on a larger scale, but I never thought to ask for more from the actual designer. I simply assumed they were the result of a design team's efforts."

"If you're saying all of this just to be nice or to butter me up for something, please don't tell me the truth yet," she murmured, letting her eyes slide closed on the riot of sensations washing through her. "Let me savor this feeling just a while longer."

Eyes still closed, she smelled Alex moving closer a second before she felt his warm breath fan her face. His aftershave was an intoxicating mix of spicy citrus and sandalwood that she remembered intimately from their single night together. Now, as she had then, she inhaled deeply, wanting to absorb his scent and carry it with her from that moment on.

His mouth pressed against hers. Soft, but firm. Passionate, but not at all inappropriate given their current location and how large an audience they might be attracting.

He pulled away long before she was ready, leaving her cold and lonely. Her eyes fluttered open and she almost moaned with disappointment.

Still standing close enough to draw undue attention, he whispered quietly, "I meant every word. Although I do have a question for you that you might think I *was* buttering you up for."

His thumbs stroked the pulse points at her wrists, which she was sure were pounding harder than a jackhammer.

"For the record, I wasn't. You can say no, even though I sincerely hope you'll say yes."

Yes. Yes, yes, yes! She didn't even know what the question was yet, but the word raced through her mind, anyway, rapidly multiplying like furry little bunnies. She almost didn't care what he asked— Will you marry me? Will you sneak into the ladies' room and let me take you against the vanity? Would you like brown sugar on your oatmeal?—she wanted to say yes.

Her voice cracked as she made herself say, "All right. What is it?"

So many words. And she sounded so reasonable, when inside she was flailing around like a passenger on a tilt-a-whirl.

"Will you come home with me?"

Some fragment of her brain thought that was a silly question.

"I have to," she told him. "You're making me stay with you until the paternity results come back."

His lips curved in a patient smile. "No," he said softly. "You know what I mean. Let me take you home, to my bed. Spend the night with me the way I've been wanting you to since you came."

She nearly wept. Inside she actually whimpered. If he only knew how hard it had been to lie in bed all those nights, alone, knowing he was only two doors away. She'd thought about him, fantasized about him, even cursed him. And then, once she'd fallen asleep, she'd dreamed about him.

"What about your fundraiser?" she asked, needing to buy a little time for her heart to slow its frantic gallop and her mind to be sure—really, really sure—she could deal with the consequences of her answer.

"There are others here who can see it through to the end. And if we don't get out of here soon, it's possible they'll be in for more of an evening than they bargained for. We're talking full-out, triple-X public displays of affection right here in the middle of the ballroom."

He emphasized his point by pressing against her, letting her feel the full state of his arousal through his tuxedo slacks and the fall of her gown. She leaned into him, reveling in his palpable desire for her. Though her response wasn't nearly as noticeable, it was just as intense, just as overwhelming.

She also wasn't sure she'd mind if he threw her down on the nearest banquet table and had his wicked way with her, but it might turn into a public relations nightmare for his people.

"Then maybe it would be best if we left," she murmured.

She felt his chest hitch as he sucked in a breath.

"Is that a yes?" he asked, his voice sounding like sandpaper on stone.

"Yes," she answered easily. "It's definitely a yes."

She wanted to laugh at the endearing, lopsided grin he beamed at her. And then they were moving. He spun her around, keeping her in front of him as he steered her across the room, making excuses and lining up others to oversee the rest of the fundraiser in his place. Depending on who he spoke to, he blamed their premature exit either on *his* early meeting schedule the next morning or *her* phantom headache.

Finally they were in his limo, pulling away from the hotel portico and racing toward his estate.

As soon as the chauffeur had closed the door behind them, Alex was on her, devouring her mouth, running his hand up and down her leg through the slit in her gown, anchoring her to him with an arm around her back.

Her fingers were in his hair, loving the silky texture and holding him in place while her tongue tangled with his. The plush leather of the wide seat cushioned them and brushed against the bare skin of her shoulders and back, making her realize they'd left the benefit without a thought for the coats they'd checked at the beginning of the evening or the chill in the late-night air.

Breaking the kiss, Alex panted for breath, his hands never pausing in their rabid exploration of her body through the sleek material of her gown.

"I want to take you right here," he grated, "so I'll never again be able to ride in this car without thinking of you."

Her heart did a little flip. "Then what are you waiting for?" she asked in a soft voice. Thankfully the privacy window was up—and she hoped soundproof.

His teeth clicked together, a muscle throbbing in his jaw. "Not enough time," he bit out. "But soon. Believe me—very soon."

With that, he pulled away, tugging her down to lie almost flat along the wide seat.

"What are you—?" she started to ask, but his hands were beneath her skirt, finding the elastic waistband of her panties.

In one swift, flawless motion, he had them down her legs and off. Then he was pushing aside the folds of the dress, leaving her naked from the belly button down except for the diamond-studded heels strapped to her feet.

Sliding to the limousine floor, he knelt there, a wolfish grin slashing his face and flashing straight white teeth. His hands at her hips tugged her forward, then gently parted her knees.

A quiver of anticipation rushed over her, pooling low in her belly. "Alex—" she whispered in a halfhearted protest, but it was already too late.

Lowering his head, he brushed kisses along the insides of

both thighs, leading upward until he reached her mound and pressed one there, as well. His lips moved over her, nuzzling the sensitive flesh and burrowing between her damp folds swollen with arousal.

He tortured her with long, slow strokes of his tongue that made her back arch and her nails dig into the leather seat cushions. She whimpered, writhed, panted for breath. Alex merely hummed his approval and redoubled his efforts to drive her out of her mind.

He licked and nibbled, flicked and suckled until Jessica wanted to scream. She was pretty sure *that* sound wouldn't remain on this side of the privacy window, however, so she squeezed her eyes shut and bit her lips until she tasted blood.

A second later, the limousine started uphill, rolling them together even tighter and pressing Alex more fully between her legs. His lips and tongue and fingers hit just the right spot with just the right amount of pressure to make her shatter, her insides coming apart in sharp, mind-blowing spasms of pleasure.

When she regained consciousness—because she truly believed she might have fainted from pure physical delight—Alex was hovering over her, smiling like a cat who'd just figured out how to unlock the birdcage. Her legs were demurely draped across his lap, her dress rearranged to cover them.

"We're home," he said quietly, leaning in to brush his fingers through her hair, which she was pretty sure was a tangled mess by now, no longer pinned in the lovely swept-up twist she'd fought so hard to get right only hours before.

With his help, she sat up, struggling to get her bearings and stop her cheeks from flushing bright red with awkwardness. It didn't help that the front of Alex's pants were noticeably tented by the bulge of his erection.

Spotting the direction of her gaze, he chuckled, shifting

slightly to alleviate the pressure behind his zipper. Then he reached down and plucked a scrap of sheer blue fabric from the car floor.

She held out her hand, expecting him to return the lost article of clothing. Instead, he dangled it from one finger, continuing to grin.

"Alex, those are my underwear," she said on a harsh whisper. Not that anyone else was around to hear. "Give them back."

"Nope."

She made a grab for them, but he slipped them into the pocket of his tuxedo jacket before she even got close. Sliding across the seat, he opened the door and stepped out, reaching a hand back to help her out.

"Come on. Let's go inside before Javier asks what all that screaming was about."

Fifteen

"Oh, no," Jessica groaned in utter mortification.

Taking his hand, she followed him to the house as fast as she could, making a concerted effort not to look around for fear she'd make eye contact with Alex's driver and die of humiliation right there on the front drive.

Once inside, he slammed the door shut, then spun her around to press her back flat to the thick wooden panel. His body boxed her in, arms braced on either side of her head, chest and hips and upper thighs pressing against her like a big, warm, heavy blanket.

His mouth crashed down on hers, stealing her breath and reviving every sensual, red-blooded nerve ending in her body, even the ones she'd thought had gotten their fair dose of pleasure for the night. She gripped the lapels of his jacket, hanging on for dear life while their tongues mated and their lips clashed hard enough to bruise.

One minute she was standing upright, pressed to the front

door. The next she was biting off a yelp of surprise as he swept an arm behind her knees, placed another at her back and yanked her off her feet.

Reluctantly, he pulled his mouth from hers and turned to march up the stairs. He carried her as though she weighed no more than Henry, but still she could feel his heart pounding beneath the layers of tuxedo jacket and dress shirt.

She kept one hand flattened there on his chest, the other toying with the short strands of hair at his nape. All the while she pressed light butterfly kisses to his cheek, his jawline, his ear, the corner of his eye, the pulse at his neck.

He growled low in his throat. She gave a long purr in response.

Stopping in the middle of the hallway, he gave a sigh that had her lifting her head. They were standing only a few feet away from the nursery door, which was slightly ajar.

"As much as it pains me," he said, "I don't want you to blame me later for not letting you see Henry before we go to bed. Especially since I intend to keep you there for a very long time. Do you want to run in and check on him?"

Her body might be humming, her blood so hot it was close to boiling her alive, but she was still a mother, and she really did want to see the baby one last time before Alex made her forget her own name.

"Would you mind?" she asked, lips twisted in apology.

He made a face. One that told her he didn't want to waste even a second on anything but getting her naked and between the sheets. But just as she'd always known, he was a good man. A kind, generous, sometimes selfless man.

Without a word, he slowly lowered her to the floor until she was standing none too steadily on her own two, three-inch-heeled feet. Keeping a hand at the small of her back, he walked with her to the nursery door.

Pushing it open, she tiptoed inside. Wendy was sitting

in the rocking chair in one corner, reading beneath the low wattage of the only lamp in the room. She lifted her head and smiled when she saw them.

"How was he tonight?" Jessica whispered, continuing over to the crib. Henry was on his back on the zoo animal sheets, covered almost to his chin by a lightweight baby blanket.

"He was an absolute angel," the nanny said, moving to Jessica's side. "We played most of the evening. I read him a story and gave him a bottle around eight. He's been sleeping ever since."

"That's great," Jessica replied, even though she was a little disappointed he wasn't still awake so she could wish him good-night. Doing the next best thing, she kissed the tips of two fingers then touched them to his tiny cheek. His mouth moved as though starting to smile—or more likely to give an extra suck of his pacifier—and warmth washed through her.

Straightening away from the side of the crib, Jessica thanked Wendy. "You can go to bed now," she told her. "I'm sure he'll be fine for a few more hours, at least."

The nanny nodded and moved back to the rocker to gather her things.

Standing close, having looked into the crib at Henry himself, Alex said, "Keep the monitor with you, if you would, please. We'll be available if you need us for anything, of course, but we'd prefer not to be disturbed tonight, if at all possible."

Jessica was sure that his hand at her waist and the high color riding her cheekbones left nothing to the nanny's imagination.

But she nodded without blinking an eye. "Of course. Not a problem, sir."

"Thank you," Alex murmured, applying pressure to Jessica's waist to get her moving toward the door.

"Thank you," Jessica said again, casting one last glance

over her shoulder at both the nanny and what she could see of the baby through the slats of the crib. "Good night."

And then she was back in the hall, being hustled next door to Alex's bedroom. She laughed at his speed and single-minded determination as he shoved her inside, catching a quick glimpse of dark wood, a masculine color palette and sprawling space before he closed the door, shutting out the light from the hall and locking them in near darkness.

As soon as they were alone, he was on her like a bird of prey, holding her face in both of his hands while he kissed her and kissed her and kissed her, turning her round and round and round as he walked her in circles farther into the room.

"Wait," she breathed between tiny nips and full-bodied thrusts of his tongue. "Turn on the lights. I want to see your room."

"Later."

"But…"

"Later," he growled.

She started to smile in amusement, but then his hands skimmed up the length of her spine, found the miniscule tab of the gown's zipper and slid it all the way down. The billowy, strapless blue material fell away from her breasts and dropped to the floor in a soft whoosh.

Since the dress didn't allow for a bra, and her panties were currently tucked in the pocket of Alex's jacket, the action left her completely naked but for her strappy stilettos and all four pieces of priceless Bajoran jewelry. Cool air washed over her, cooling the diamonds against her skin, raising gooseflesh and pebbling her nipples.

Or maybe it was the anticipation of making love with Alex again after what seemed like forever.

He stepped back, his eagle eyes roaming over her nude-but-bejeweled form from head to toe. Though how he could see much of anything in the dark, she didn't know. Only the faint glow of moonlight shone through the sheer curtains at the windows.

Not that the lack of illumination seemed to bother him. Not letting it slow him down one tiny bit, he shrugged out of his tuxedo jacket and started to undo his tie, collar and cuff links.

One by one, items were discarded, the buttons at the front of his starched white shirt slipped through their holes. Slowly, the hard planes of his chest came into view. Shadows of them, at any rate.

Heart rapping, she closed the scrap of distance between them, covering his hands at the waist of his slacks. His movements stilled and she pushed his hands away entirely.

He let them fall to his sides, giving up so easily. Yet she could feel the tension emanating from his body, in the steel-cable rigidity of his stance and every tightly held muscle.

His chest rose and fell in sharp cadence as she tugged the tails of his shirt out of the waistband of his pants. Pushing the fabric open and off over his shoulders, she let her palms run the full expanse of his wide masculine chest.

Just as she remembered from so long ago, it was broad and smooth, throwing off heat like a furnace. A light sprinkling of hair tickled her fingertips while she explored his flat abdomen; the rise of his pectorals with their rough, peaked centers; the hard jut of his collarbones and the curve of his strong shoulders.

The white material floated to the floor, and she returned her hands to the front of his pants. Sliding them open, she lowered the zipper past his straining erection while he sucked in a harsh breath and held it. She let her knuckles brush along his length through his black silk boxers.

Muttering a curse, he kicked out of his shoes, stripped the slacks and underwear down his muscular legs, and dragged her away from the entire pile of their shed clothing. He

walked them over to the large four-poster bed, lifting her
onto the end of the high mattress.

He moved in for a kiss, tipping her chin up and cupping
her face in both hands. His thumbs gently brushed the line
of her jaw while he drank from her mouth. She parted her
knees, making room for him in the cradle of her thighs, and
he pressed close, brushing every part of her with every part
of him.

Her nails dug into the meat at the sides of his waist, then
she brought her legs up to hitch her knees over his hips. He
groaned, the sound filling her mouth as he leaned into her
even more.

A second later she found herself lifted by her buttocks and
tossed several inches closer to the center of the bed. Alex
came with her, landing on top of her even as she bounced
lightly, the glossy satin coverlet cool at her back.

While she wrapped her legs more firmly around him, he
buried his face in her neck and began trailing kisses down her
throat, tracing the lines of the necklace until it gave way to
the bare flesh of her chest and one plump breast. He pressed
his mouth dead center, then started to lick and nip all around.

Beneath him, Jessica arched, moaned, writhed. And Alex
reveled in every ripple, every soft whimper of sound.

He'd wanted to drape her in his jewels, and now he had.
And she was just as glorious as he'd known she would be
in nothing but what he'd borrowed from the company safe.

He could hardly believe he actually had her in his bed
again.

Different bed. Different city and state. Different year.
Maybe even two different people…different than they'd been
the first time around, anyway.

But so much was the same. The instant spark between
them that quickly turned into a five-alarm fire. The uncon-

trollable desire he felt for her almost every minute of every day. Her hot, liquid response to his touch.

She humbled him and made him feel like a superhero all at once. And it was quite possible she'd given him a son. An heir. Another Bajoran to someday take over the family business.

That thought made him want to put her up on a pedestal and treat her like a queen. Surround her in swaths of cotton and bubble wrap, and keep her safe for the rest of their lives.

But for now, with her warm and willing beneath him, he most wanted to drive her to the brink and then straight over the edge into mind-bending bliss.

If only he could hold back his own climax long enough to get her there. And the way her legs were wrapped around his hips, her damp heat brushing him in all the right places, was making that more and more impossible.

Her stiff nipple abraded his tongue as he swiped at it over and over again. Around it, her dusky rose flesh puckered and tightened.

With a groan, he moved to her other breast and did the same. Her hands stroked his bare back, his shoulders, through his hair and along his scalp. Her nails scraped and dug and clawed.

Between her legs her warmth beckoned. He burrowed closer, locking his jaw to keep from moaning aloud. Continuing to toy with her nipples and the sensitive area surrounding them, he trailed his hands down her sides, over her hips and the mound of her femininity. She gasped as his fingers found her, and he captured the sound with his mouth.

For long languorous minutes, he explored her feminine core. The soft folds, swollen channel and tight, sensitive bud, all slick with tantalizing moisture.

"Alex, please," she whimpered against his lips, her pelvis rising upward, straining for the pleasure he was so cruelly withholding.

As much as he wanted to keep playing, keep touching and stroking and teasing her for hours on end, he didn't have all that much restraint left, either. Not after a year of celibacy since their last time together and the torturous session in the limousine.

Sliding more closely against her, he let her wet heat engulf him as he slowly pressed forward. He gritted his teeth while she took him inch by inch, her chest hitching beneath him in an effort to continue taking in oxygen. His own lungs burned just like hers, every muscle bunching tight.

"I remember this, you know," he grated, nostrils flaring and mind racing while he tried desperately to distract himself from the incredible sensations threatening to make him come apart at the seams.

She made a sound low in her throat. Part agreement, part desperation.

"I never forgot," he told her, "even though I tried hard to do just that."

Jessica's breath blew out on a shuddering sigh. "Alex?"

"Hmm?"

"Let's talk later, okay?"

She panted the words, her nails curling into his shoulder blades and making him shudder from the top of his scalp to the soles of his feet.

He chuckled. "Okay."

Grasping her about the waist, he yanked her toward him as he thrust, driving himself to the hilt. She gasped, and Alex ground his teeth to keep from doing the same.

Rolling them both to their sides, he held her there, moving inside of her, kissing her while temperatures rose, sensations built and the air filled with the sounds of heavy breathing and needy mewls. Jessica's hands on his body licked like flames. Tiny flicks of pleasure that shot straight to his center.

They rocked together on the soft, wide mattress. Side to side. Forward and back. Tongues mingled while bodies meshed, slowly becoming one. Her hips rose to meet his every thrust, her breasts rubbing his chest.

"Alex," she whispered, pulling her mouth from his to suck in a heartfelt breath. "Please."

She didn't need to beg. He was right there with her, desperate and so close to going over, his bones ached.

Clasping her smooth, bare buttocks, he tugged her closer, then rolled them again so that she was on her back and he was above her, covering her like a blanket. Faster and faster they moved until she was clenching around him and he was straining not to explode.

Which would have been a lot easier if she weren't grabbing at his hair and murmuring, "Yes, yes, please, yes," over and over again in his ear.

"Jessica," he bit out, not sure how much longer he could hold out.

"Alex," she returned with equal urgency. "Alex, please. Now."

"Yes," he agreed, forcing the word past his locked jaw. "Now."

And then he was breaking apart with Jessica spasming around him, her cries of delight filling the room and echoing in his ears.

Sixteen

Jessica stretched and rolled to her opposite side, surprised to find herself alone in the wide king-size bed. All through the night, Alex hadn't let her get more than half an inch from him except to run to the bathroom or peek in on Henry.

He'd wrapped his arms around her, tugged her snug against his long solid frame and held her while they slept. Then he'd woken her with kisses and the light caress of his hands on her skin to make love to her again. And once she'd awakened him the same way.

As nights went, it had been just about perfect.

Finding herself alone with the midmorning sunlight shining through the curtains put a bit of a damper on that perfection, though. It made her wonder if the entire evening had been as wonderful as she remembered. If the feelings she'd felt for Alex and *thought* he might return were real.

Insecurities flooding her, she slipped from the bed, pulling the rumpled coverlet along to tuck over her breasts, letting it trail behind her like a long train. She gathered her dress and shoes and other personal items from the seat of a chair where Alex had apparently collected them from the floor. Checking the hall, she tiptoed to her room and dressed in something other than an evening gown and three-inch heels.

With her hair pulled back in a loose ponytail and her body encased in comfortable cotton and denim, she headed for Henry's nursery only to find the crib empty. Far from being worried, she simply assumed he was with the nanny.

Making her way downstairs, Jessica checked Alex's office first, wanting to see him again, even though she wasn't entirely sure how he would respond to her in the bright light of day. But the room was empty, the door standing wide open and Alex's chair pushed back from his desk.

Turning toward the other side of the house, she trailed along to the kitchen, deciding that even if she didn't find Alex or Wendy and Henry there, she could at least grab a bite of breakfast.

As soon as she stepped into the deluxe gargantuan room, she heard the sounds of her son's giggles over the gentle din of pots and pans, spoons and spatulas. Alex sat in the breakfast nook before the wide bank of tall windows with Henry balanced on one strong thigh.

He was dressed more casually than she'd ever seen him in a pair of simple tan slacks and a white dress shirt open at the collar. Henry had a bib tucked under his chin, and there were small dishes of assorted baby foods on the table in front of them. Alex was obviously attempting to feed him, but he must have been teasing too much because Henry couldn't stop laughing and wiggling around.

Slipping her fingers into the front pockets of her jeans, Jessica strolled to the table. She was a little nervous after what she and Alex had shared last night, but happy, too, to see him so friendly and comfortable with the baby.

"What are you two up to?" she asked in a near singsong voice, sliding onto the bench seat across the table from them.

Raising his head, Alex shot her a wide grin, a spoonful of orange goop—peaches, she assumed—hanging from his free hand.

"Just letting you sleep a little longer," he replied. "And getting to know my son a bit better."

He said it so easily, so casually that she almost didn't catch his meaning. Then the words sank in and her eyes snapped to his.

Her sharp gaze must have been questioning enough, because he gave an almost imperceptible nod. "The doctor called this morning. The test results are positive—Henry is most definitely mine."

Jessica almost couldn't hear for the sound of her heart pounding in her ears. She'd never doubted Henry's paternity, of course—she *knew* Alex was the father for the simple fact that there'd been no other men in her life at the time of his conception…as well as long before and after. But she'd nearly forgotten Alex's doubts, and that DNA results were what they'd both been waiting around for.

Taking a moment to mentally slow her rampant pulse, she swallowed and then cocked both her head and a single brow. "Am I allowed to say *I told you so?* Because I *did* tell you so."

To her surprise, he chuckled, a genuine smile breaking out across his normally stern features. "Yes, you did." His smile slipping a couple of notches, he added, "I hope you know I wanted to believe you. I wanted it to be true, I just… I had to be sure."

His heavy-lidded eyes were storm-cloud blue and almost— she could have sworn—apologetic. She did understand. Alex alone was worth millions of dollars, his family as a group likely worth hundreds of millions. For all she knew, dozens of women had shown up on his doorstep claiming he was the father of their children.

Her own father had run off many a young man he suspected was more interested in the Taylor fortune than in her. It had made dating in high school an adolescent nightmare.

"So what do we do now?" she asked quietly.

Before Alex could answer, Mrs. Sheppard appeared at her elbow, sliding a plate of scrambled eggs and toast in front of her. She added a glass of orange juice and then disappeared again to the other side of the room, well out of earshot.

"Are you going to eat?" Alex asked after she'd sat there a few long minutes staring at the meal but making no move to touch it.

Taking a deep breath, she picked up her fork and stabbed at the eggs but turned her true attention to him instead.

"I'm a little distracted right now," she told him.

"For good reason, I suppose," he said, inclining his head and taking a moment to feed Henry another spoonful of pureed baby breakfast.

"I need to run into the office for a while this morning, but was hoping you'd meet me there later. Do you think you could do that—and bring Henry with you?"

"A-all right," she stuttered, confused by his nonchalance and focus on a topic unrelated to the recent discovery that he was, indeed, Henry's father. "But what about—"

Pushing to his feet, he carried Henry over to her and deposited the baby into her arms instead. Henry giggled, kicked and wiggled until she got him arranged on her own lap. Alex moved the jars of baby food to her side of the table and handed her the tiny peach-caked spoon.

"Just meet me at my office in a couple of hours, okay? Around one o'clock."

He leaned down and pressed a kiss to the crown of her head, ruffling the top of Henry's at the same time.

"Trust me," he added.

Calmly, competently, completely at ease while her insides were jumping around like seltzer water.

Two hours later, almost on the dot, Jessica walked into the Bajoran Designs office building. She wasn't sneaking around this time, hoping to get in and out without being spotted by security. Instead, Alex had made sure a car and driver were available to bring her into the city and drop her off at the front door.

She'd also changed from jeans and casual top to a short burgundy wraparound dress, and put Henry into a long-sleeve shirt covered in cute yellow ducks with a pair of brown corduroy overalls. She didn't know what Alex's intentions were for asking her to come to his office with the baby, but she wanted to be prepared. And knowing she looked good helped to boost her self-confidence.

At least that's what she told herself as she made her way up to the twelfth floor in the main elevator. The doors slid open and she stepped out.

She was a little surprised to find the reception desk and hallway completely empty on a Wednesday afternoon. Not even a receptionist behind the main desk. If the place had been this deserted when she'd left Henry on Alex's boardroom table, she wouldn't have had nearly as much trouble sneaking in and out or been half as nervous about getting caught.

Since Henry's carrier—with Henry strapped safely inside—was getting heavy, she set him on the low coffee table in the waiting area, wondering if she should stay here or go in search of Alex.

Before she could decide for sure, a door opened at the end of the long hallway and voices filtered out. A minute later Alex stepped into view, standing aside while several other men, also dressed in expensive, conservative suits, filed out. The last man exited the room, flanked by two security officers.

He wasn't handcuffed. In fact, they weren't touching him at all. But it was clear they were escorting him, and he looked none too happy about it.

Jessica stayed where she was, watching as the group of men made their way to the elevators, waited for the car to arrive and stepped on. The second elevator carried the angry man and the two security guards to the lobby.

After both sets of doors slid closed, she turned her head to find Alex striding toward her, a warm smile softening the strong lines of his face. From the moment he'd issued the invitation, she hadn't known what to expect. That look encouraged her, made her think they might be here for something other than bad news.

"You came," he said, leaning in to press a light kiss to her mouth. He stroked a hand down her bare arm to thread his fingers with hers at the same time he patted Henry's leg and sent the carrier rocking back and forth.

"You asked us to," Jessica replied carefully, not quite sure what else to say.

"And you trusted me enough to do it, even though I didn't tell you why I wanted you here."

He seemed infinitely pleased by that fact, and she found herself returning his near grin.

"I have a surprise for you," he said. "But first we need to talk."

"All right."

He gestured for her to take a seat on the low leather sofa, then sat down beside her. Their knees brushed, and he reached for her other hand so that he held both of hers in both of his, resting on his upper thigh.

Inside her chest, her heart bounced against her ribs, her

diaphragm tightening with nerves. She had no idea what he was going to say, but she felt like a teenager about to be reprimanded for missing curfew.

"I looked into the problem you mentioned about your family," he told her. When her brows came together in a frown, he clarified. "The belief that Taylor Fine Jewels was forced out of partnership with Bajoran Designs."

She understood what he was talking about, but was no less confused.

"It turns out you were right. For the record," he was quick to point out, "I knew nothing about it. All of that was over and done with before I took over the position of CEO, and behind my father's back. But my cousin George apparently decided he could rise higher and bring in more money for the Bajorans if our two families were no longer in business together."

Jessica's eyes widened. She wasn't all that stunned by Alex's pronouncement, considering she'd known the truth all along. Maybe not the details—about his cousin being the impetus for her family's ruin—but she'd certainly known the rest.

What surprised her was that Alex had listened to her and looked into her claims rather than automatically taking his family's side and dismissing her as crazy or scorned.

"Thank you," she said with a small hitch in her voice.

Knowing what Alex had done—that he'd discovered the truth and was man enough to admit it—suddenly meant the world to her.

It was so much more than she would have expected of anyone…but especially Alex.

"Don't thank me," he said with a shake of his head. "Not when I owe you an apology. What my cousin did was wrong and is what started all the bad blood."

Jessica gave a watery chuckle. "It seems we both have evil cousins hiding in the branches of our family trees. What I did to you back in Portland thanks to *my* cousin was wrong and unfair to you, as well. If you can forgive me for that, I think I can forgive you for something you had absolutely nothing to do with."

Lifting a hand to his lips, he kissed her fingers. "I forgive you," he murmured in a tone so resolved she could never doubt his sincerity.

"I forgave you long ago," he continued, "though I'm not sure I realized it until recently. But I owe you—and your family—more than that."

She started to shake her head. "You don't owe me—" she began, but he cut her off with a smile and the pad of one index finger pressed to her lips.

"It's already done, so just sit there for a minute and let me tell you how I'm making this right."

She swallowed hard, taken aback by his determination on the subject. But she did as he asked, sitting back and giving a short nod to let him finish.

"The man you saw being led out by security…that was my cousin George. The others were board members who came in for an emergency shareholders meeting. Once I explained to them what George had done and showed them definitive proof, they agreed to his immediate termination."

His lips twisted at her shocked gasp. "He only went quietly under threat of having criminal charges leveled against him."

"I can't believe you would fire your own cousin," she whispered.

Alex scowled. "He's lucky I didn't throttle him. I might yet. But that doesn't do much to help your family, so I want you to know that I intend to approach them about going into business with us once again."

Jessica's lungs hitched, her pulse skipping a beat. "Oh, Alex," she breathed.

"Do you think it's something they'll go for?"

"There may be hard feelings at first," she said with a laugh. "The Taylors can certainly be stubborn at times. But once they've had a chance to consider your offer and realize it's genuine, I think they'll be delighted."

On a burst of pure gladness she bounced off the sofa cushion and threw herself against Alex's chest, hugging him tight. "You really are a wonderful man, Alexander Bajoran. Thank you."

His arms wrapped around her, squeezing her back. He cleared his throat before speaking, but even then his voice was rough.

"You're welcome. There's more, though," he said, giving her one last embrace before setting her away from him and taking her hands again.

His chest swelled as he took a deep breath. This next part was delicate. She was either going to be thrilled with him and throw herself into his arms again, or she was going to be furious and possibly slap him a good one.

"Your parents are here," he announced quickly—almost too quickly, like tearing off a bandage. He saw the question in her eyes, the incomprehension on her face.

"What? Why are they... What?"

Mouth dry and pulse racing, Alex tightened his grip on her fingers. "I'm hoping you'll consider sticking around Seattle for a while longer, preferably staying with me so that we can see if this...*thing* between us is as real and as strong as it feels. And in order to do that, your parents need to know where you are—and that they have a grandson."

He'd crossed the line in contacting Jessica's parents behind her back and without her permission, but he hadn't known how else to get all of their problems ironed out and taken care of in one fell swoop. And for some reason it was important to him to get everything out in the open and dealt with *right now*.

There had been too many secrets, too many lies already. Starting years ago with his cousin's slimy, despicable actions toward her family on behalf of his, to as early as this morning when the doctor had called and announced that he *was* indeed Henry's biological father.

That phone call had both elated and disgraced him.

Elated him because he couldn't imagine anything that would make him happier than knowing Henry was his. Especially after last night when he'd pretty much decided he didn't care one way or the other.

Being with Jessica again, in and out of bed, had reignited the same powerful feelings he'd felt for her a year ago, and he'd known he wanted to keep her in his life. Jessica and Henry both, regardless of DNA.

But the test results had shamed him, too, because they reminded him that he'd doubted Jessica to begin with. Doubted her word, doubted her integrity, let pride and suspicions cloud what his heart and gut had been trying to tell him.

Hadn't he known as soon as he'd seen her again that he was in love with her? Hadn't he known the minute she'd told him Henry was his son that she'd been telling the truth?

She'd made some bad decisions, but he had some making up to do, that was for sure. And today's business was a step in that direction.

Still clutching Jessica's hands in his lap, he stroked her long slim fingers distractedly.

"I told them everything. Explained how we met last year, how you tried to steal company secrets to avenge the wrong that had been done to your family. And I told them about Henry."

With each word he uttered, Jessica's eyes grew wider, her expression panicked while the color leeched from her skin. On his lap her hands started to quiver.

"I'm sorry," he told her quickly. "I know it was probably

your place to tell them about the baby and why you disappeared on them, but I didn't want them to feel ambushed once they arrived. And I sort of hoped that having time to think during the flight—" he'd sent his own jet to pick them up "—would help them absorb the turn of events more easily."

"Oh, God," Jessica groaned, dropping her head to rest on their clasped hands. She was breathing fast and shallow... he hoped *not* on the verge of hyperventilating.

"Oh, God, oh, God. What did they say?" she asked in a muffled voice. "Were they angry? Do they hate me? Did my mother cry? I can't handle it when my mother cries. Oh, they must be *so* upset and disappointed in me."

Her hysterics were enough to make him chuckle, but he very wisely held back. Instead, he freed a hand to rub his wide palm up and down the line of her spine.

"Your mother did cry," he said, remembering his meeting with them in his office before he'd crossed the hall to deal with his cousin and the board.

"But I'm pretty sure they were happy tears. She's delighted to have a grandson, and can't wait to see him. They're eager to see you again, too, though your father did admit that if you'd shown up pregnant with my child, they probably would have been none too pleased. Realizing how they likely would have reacted to the news helped them to understand why you've stayed away these past months, I think."

Taking a deep, shuddering breath, Jessica raised her head and met his gaze. Her eyes were damp and worried.

"Do you really think so?"

He gave her a reassuring smile. "I do. Your parents are very nice people," he added. "I liked them, and am looking forward to working with them if they agree to partner with Bajoran Designs again."

The anxiety in her features seemed to fade as she reached

up to stroke his cheek. "You're something else, you know that?"

Alex quirked a brow. "In a good way or a bad way?"

"Oh, a very good way. I might even go so far as to say amazing, but I don't want you to get an inflated opinion of yourself. Or more of one, at any rate," she teased.

Then she sobered again. "I mean it, Alex. What you've done, all of it, it's…wonderful. And you didn't have to. You didn't have to do any of it. I'd have told my parents everything eventually. And what happened between our families, with the company… It was so long ago, and you had nothing to do with it. You could have let it all go on just as it has been."

"No," he said with a sharp shake of his head and the beginning of a scowl, "I couldn't. I don't want either of us to go into this relationship with baggage."

Jessica licked her lips, eyes darting to the side before returning to his.

"Relationship?" she asked in little more than a whisper.

"Yes." His tone was low, serious. Because this was possibly the most serious, important conversation of his life.

"I meant what I said," he continued, being sure to hold her gaze. "I want you to stay. Move in with me officially, as more than just a temporary guest. I'd really like to see if we can make this work. As a couple. As a family."

For several tense seconds she didn't respond. Except to blink, her thick lashes fluttering over wide eyes.

She was silent for so long, Alex nearly squirmed. Maybe this had been a bad idea. Maybe he was pushing for too much too soon.

As usual he'd forged ahead with his own plans, his own desires, expecting everyone and everything to fall into place just as he wanted it. After all, wasn't that how it had been his entire life?

This was so much more important than anything else

had ever been, though. And it wasn't only about what he wanted—it was about what Jessica wanted, and what was best for both her and Henry.

His ideal would be for them to stay with him. He didn't know if they were ready for forever just yet, but he certainly wouldn't mind if they moved in that direction.

If Jessica wanted something different, however, if her ideal was something else entirely, then he would have to accept that. He would still be in Henry's life, there was no doubt about that. And he didn't think Jessica would ever try to keep him out of it.

When the near-static buzz of intense silence became oddly uncomfortable, Alex cleared his throat and made a concerted effort to loosen his grip on Jessica's fingers. As romantic and sweeping as he'd hoped his actions and this gesture would be, it was a lot to digest. He couldn't blame her for being wary and needing time to consider her options.

"It's all right if you're not ready for something like that," he told her. He kept his tone even, devoid of the disappointment churning in his gut. "I shouldn't have sprung everything on you quite so quickly. I understand if you need time to think it through. And maybe last night was just one of those things. It didn't have to mean anything—"

The pads of two fingers pressed to his lips stopped him midsentence.

"It meant something," she said, barely above a whisper. "And I don't need time to decide anything. Yes—Henry and I would love to move in with you. Your house—mausoleum that it is—" she added with a grin "—is starting to feel like home already. I'm just…surprised you're asking. I'm shocked by all of this," she admitted, leaning slightly away from him and sweeping her arms out to encompass the waiting area and beyond.

Turning back to him, her eyes were warm, her expression

open and inviting. It made his heart swell and his own blood heat to a healthy temperature as it pumped through his veins.

"But, Alex," she began, her voice quietly controlled, "are you sure about this? You were so unconvinced of Henry's paternity, so suspicious of me. I didn't think you felt...*that way* about me."

She wasn't trying to make him feel like a heel, but he did. And if he'd ever needed confirmation that she was one of the most honest, genuine women he'd ever met—*not* a gold digger after his or his family's fortune—her cautious protests would have done it.

With a grin he felt straight to his bones, he brought her knuckles to his lips and kissed them gently. "Maybe I wasn't convincing enough last night."

"Oh, you were plenty convincing. But that's just sex, Alex. What you're talking about is...more. At least if you're saying what I think you're saying."

"I am," he told her. No hesitation, no mincing words. "It was definitely more than just sex between us. Last night and a year ago—I think you know that. From the moment we met," he murmured, alternately brushing the tops of her fingers and the underside of her wrists, "there was something between us. I'm just asking now for a chance to make it work. To see if we have a future together."

A short, shaky laugh rolled up from her throat. "I'd like that. More than you can imagine."

Yanking her to her feet, he held her close and kissed her until they were both gasping for breath.

"I'd like to take you home right now and celebrate properly," he told her, hands tangled in the hair at either side of her head while he cradled her face. "But your parents are still waiting in my office, no doubt growing more agitated by the minute. I know they're eager to see you...not to mention meet their grandson for the first time."

She inhaled deeply, then let the air slip from her lungs in a quavering sigh. "Will you come with us? I don't want to do this alone."

Rubbing his thumb along the full swell of her lower lip, he smiled gently. "You don't ever have to be alone again."

Epilogue

One Year Later...

The ballroom was brimming with guests dressed in tuxedos and designer gowns. Their voices were a loud din, interspersed by laughter and the clinking of glasses.

Beside her, Alex smiled and nodded as an associate droned on about his recent vacation in Milan, while the butterflies in Jessica's stomach fluttered violently enough to break through and fly away.

She tried to pay attention, really she did. And her cheeks hurt from trying to keep such a pleasant smile on her face. Inside, though, she was shaking, her fingers cold and stiff around her flute of champagne.

Apparently noticing her silent distress, Alex wrapped up his conversation with the couple before them and took her elbow to lead her several feet away. There weren't many quiet corners in the overflowing ballroom, but he managed to find one.

"You look like you're going to pass out," he remarked, clearly amused. His hands moved up and down her bare arms, rubbing warmth back into them along with a semblance of normalcy.

"Take a deep breath," he commanded. "Now slow and easy. Relax. You're the guest of honor tonight...you should be walking on air."

She followed his instructions, *tried* to relax and was relieved to feel her pulse slow by at least a couple of beats per minute.

"What if they hate it? What if you lose money? What if they hate *me* and start hating Bajoran Designs? You know the rumor is that I trapped you for revenge, and blackmailed you into bringing my family back into the company."

He had the nerve to chuckle, which earned him a less-than-ladylike scowl.

"Only a few very shallow, catty and jealous people think that. Everyone else—everyone who counts, at any rate—thinks you're delightful and knows how lucky I am that you and your family gave me a second chance."

Continuing in her downward spiral of unladylike behavior, she snorted with disbelief.

Alex lifted a hand to her face, brushing his knuckles lightly along one cheek and into her hair, which was currently loose around her shoulders, streaks of cotton-candy-pink spiraling through the otherwise blond curls.

Another bit of ammunition the gossips relished using against her, but she liked it and Alex claimed it was "hot."

"It's true," he told her. "Just as it's true that you're magnificently talented, and your True Love Line is going to be hugely successful."

Dropping her head to his chest, she inhaled the spicy masculine scent of his cologne and fought not to cry. "I just don't want to embarrass you or make anyone at your company mad for taking a chance on me."

Thumbs beneath her jawline, he raised her gaze to his. "First, you could never embarrass me. And second, it's not *my* company. Not anymore. It's *our* company, which means you have just as much say in what takes place there as I do. Besides, everyone at Bajoran Designs knows incredible natural talent when they see it. Giving you your own line was, as they say, a no-brainer."

That brought a smile to her face, the first honest one of the evening.

"Your family is here," Alex continued. "My family is here. Even Henry is here."

He cast a glance over his shoulder to where their fifteen-month-old son—the only child in attendance—was perched on his grandmother's hip in his adorable miniature tuxedo. He was starting to pull himself up and toddle around now, eager to learn to walk so he could become even more independent and keep up with the adults in his life. Until he managed that, however, he spent his time alternately napping, charming the world or getting into trouble as only a rambunctious toddler could.

But she and Alex both adored him more each day. Even the days they fell into bed utterly exhausted from chasing him around Alex's sprawling estate.

She'd been surprised, actually, when Alex had insisted they bring the baby along tonight, despite the fact that it was well past Henry's bedtime and they were inviting public crankiness by keeping him awake. But Alex had wanted—in his words—his "entire family" there for the debut of Jessica's True Love Line. A gesture that had both touched her and filled her with added anxiety.

"All to show how proud they are and how much they support you."

Chest finally beginning to loosen, she gave a peaceful sigh. "You're better than a full body massage, do you know that?"

Alex made a low, contented sound at the back of his throat. "I'll remind you that you said that—later, when we get home."

Leaning into him, she let his warmth and love surround her, calm her, remind her why she'd been inspired to name her debut jewelry line True Love to begin with. The wisdom of that decision was only underscored when he pressed a kiss to her brow.

"At the risk of sending you into a near faint again," he murmured against her skin, "I have one more thing I need to discuss with you before we unveil your designs."

A shimmer of tension rolled through her, but nowhere near the level of moments before.

Reaching into his pocket, Alex drew out a small velvet jewelry box with the Bajoran Designs logo stamped on the outside.

"We've been together a year now. Living together, raising Henry, loving each other like a real family. And I, at least, think it's working."

Popping open the lid of the box, he held it out to her. Inside was the most beautiful, sparkling diamond engagement ring she'd ever seen. Her heart lurched and the air stuck in her lungs.

"So how about we make it official?" he asked. "I love you, Jessica. I have almost since the moment we met, even if I didn't quite realize it. You getting pregnant with Henry that first night together was the greatest miracle of my life, because it brought you back to me when I might have lost you otherwise."

Moisture prickled Jessica's eyes as emotion filled her with a wave of unadulterated joy, tightening her chest.

"Oh, Alex," she breathed. "I love you, too. And I'm so glad you saw Henry and me as a blessing rather than a burden."

He tugged her close once again, framing her face with both hands, placing a hard kiss on her lips this time. When he spoke, he had to clear his throat, and even then his voice was rough and deeper than normal.

"The only burden you or Henry could ever cause me is making me hold this ring much longer. Will you marry me, Jessica? Be my wife, my lover, my partner both at home and at the office, and the mother of not just the child we already have, but any others who might come along?"

It was the easiest question she'd ever had to answer.

"Oh, yes." A tear slipped down her cheek, and she couldn't have cared less that it might mar her perfectly applied makeup.

He took the ring from its nest of velvet and slipped it on her left hand. The stone, roughly the size of a dime, glittered in the light of the room. She turned her hand one way, then another, taking pleasure in every facet and detail that caught her eye.

"It's beautiful, Alex, thank you."

It was also huge and quite heavy. She would need a little red wagon to cart it around with her all day, every day.

"I designed it myself," he told her, chuckling when she shot him a surprised look. "I may not be as talented as you, but I knew what I wanted. I also know what you like."

Taking her hand, he slid the ring back off her finger. "I know you think it's too big, too ostentatious, even though secretly, you adore how large and showy it is."

Well, he had her there. Didn't every woman want an engagement ring the size of a compact car to show off and use to impress their friends?

"Which is why it's actually two rings that come together to form one."

He wiggled things around with a little click, and suddenly he held a piece in each hand. They were both gorgeous and still quite remarkable, while also being a bit more manageable.

"You can choose which to wear on a regular basis, or switch back and forth, if you like. And when you want to flaunt your wealth or show off just how much your husband adores you, you can put them together and cause temporary blind spells everywhere you go."

She laughed, amazed at his ingenuity and how much thought he'd put into it when he could have pulled any ring from the Bajoran Designs collection instead, and she wouldn't have known the difference.

"I'm *very* impressed," she admitted as he clicked the two bands into place and slipped all umpteen carats back on her finger.

Going on tiptoe, she wrapped her arms around his neck and pressed a soft kiss to his waiting lips. "I also love it. And I love you. Coming to Seattle was the best decision I ever made, even if we got off to a slightly rocky start."

His own arms came up to circle her waist, holding her close while he nibbled lightly at the corners of her mouth and jaw.

"Ah, but don't you know that the rockiest paths sometimes lead to the very best destinations?"

With a perfectly contented sigh, she leaned back to stare deep into his crystal-clear sapphire eyes.

"Yes, I guess I do," she whispered as everything else faded away, leaving them the only two people in the world, let alone the crowded ballroom. "Because my rocky path led me to you."

* * * * *

REQUEST YOUR FREE BOOKS!

2 FREE NOVELS PLUS 2 FREE GIFTS!

♦ Harlequin®

Desire

ALWAYS POWERFUL, PASSIONATE AND PROVOCATIVE

YES! Please send me 2 FREE Harlequin Desire® novels and my 2 FREE gifts (gifts are worth about $10). After receiving them, if I don't wish to receive any more books, I can return the shipping statement marked "cancel." If I don't cancel, I will receive 6 brand-new novels every month and be billed just $4.30 per book in the U.S. or $4.99 per book in Canada. That's a saving of at least 14% off the cover price! It's quite a bargain! Shipping and handling is just 50¢ per book in the U.S. and 75¢ per book in Canada.* I understand that accepting the 2 free books and gifts places me under no obligation to buy anything. I can always return a shipment and cancel at any time. Even if I never buy another book, the two free books and gifts are mine to keep forever.

225/326 HDN FEF3

Name	(PLEASE PRINT)

Address	Apt. #

City	State/Prov.	Zip/Postal Code

Signature (if under 18, a parent or guardian must sign)

Mail to the **Reader Service:**

IN U.S.A.: P.O. Box 1867, Buffalo, NY 14240-1867
IN CANADA: P.O. Box 609, Fort Erie, Ontario L2A 5X3

Not valid for current subscribers to Harlequin Desire books.

Want to try two free books from another line?
Call 1-800-873-8635 or visit www.ReaderService.com.

* Terms and prices subject to change without notice. Prices do not include applicable taxes. Sales tax applicable in N.Y. Canadian residents will be charged applicable taxes. Offer not valid in Quebec. This offer is limited to one order per household. All orders subject to credit approval. Credit or debit balances in a customer's account(s) may be offset by any other outstanding balance owed by or to the customer. Please allow 4 to 6 weeks for delivery. Offer available while quantities last.

Your Privacy—The Reader Service is committed to protecting your privacy. Our Privacy Policy is available online at www.ReaderService.com or upon request from the Reader Service.

We make a portion of our mailing list available to reputable third parties that offer products we believe may interest you. If you prefer that we not exchange your name with third parties, or if you wish to clarify or modify your communication preferences, please visit us at www.ReaderService.com/consumerchoice or write to us at Reader Service Preference Service, P.O. Box 9062, Buffalo, NY 14269. Include your complete name and address.

HDES11B

Harlequin® Desire is proud to present

ONE WINTER'S NIGHT

by New York Times *bestselling author*

Brenda Jackson

Alpha Blake tightened her coat around her. Not only would she be late for her appointment with Riley Westmoreland, but because of her flat tire they would have to change the location of the meeting and Mr. Westmoreland would be the one driving her there. This was totally embarrassing, when she had been trying to make a good impression.

She turned up the heat in her car. Even with a steady stream of hot air coming in through the car vents, she still felt cold, too cold, and wondered if she would ever get used to the Denver weather. Of course, it was too late to think about that now. It was her first winter here, and she didn't have any choice but to grin and bear it. When she'd moved, she'd felt that getting as far away from Daytona Beach as she could was essential to her peace of mind. But who in her right mind would prefer blistering-cold Denver to sunny Daytona Beach? Only a person wanting to start a new life and put a painful past behind her.

Her attention was snagged by an SUV that pulled off the road and parked in front of her. The door swung open and long denim-clad, boot-wearing legs appeared before a man stepped out of the truck. She met his gaze through the windshield and forgot to breathe. Walking toward her car was a man who was so dangerously masculine, so heart-stoppingly virile, that her brain went momentarily numb.

He was tall, and the Stetson on his head made him appear taller. But his height was secondary to the sharp

HDEXP1212

handsomeness of his features.

Her gaze slid all over him as he moved his long limbs toward her vehicle in a walk that was so agile and self-assured, she envied the confidence he exuded with every step. Her breasts suddenly peaked, and she could actually feel blood rushing through her veins.

She didn't have to guess who this man was.

He was Riley Westmoreland.

Find out if Riley and Alpha mix business with pleasure in

ONE WINTER'S NIGHT

by Brenda Jackson

Available December 2012

Only from Harlequin® Desire

SPECIAL EDITION

Life, Love and Family

NEW YORK TIMES BESTSELLING AUTHOR

DIANA PALMER

brings you a brand-new Western romance
featuring characters that readers have come to
love—the Brannt family from Harlequin HQN's
bestselling book *WYOMING TOUGH*.

Cort Brannt, Texas rancher through and through,
is about to unexpectedly get lassoed by love!

THE RANCHER

Available November 13 wherever books are sold!

Also available as a 2-in-1
THE RANCHER & HEART OF STONE

Harlequin® Desire

ALWAYS POWERFUL, PASSIONATE AND PROVOCATIVE.

DON'T MISS THE SEDUCTIVE CONCLUSION TO THE MINISERIES

WITH FAN-FAVORITE AUTHOR

BARBARA DUNLOP

Prince Raif Khouri believes that Waverly's high-end-auction-house executive Ann Richardson is responsible for the theft of his valuable antique Gold Heart statue, rumored to be a good luck charm to his family. The only way Raif can keep an eye on her—and get the truth from her—is by kidnapping Ann and taking her to his kingdom. But soon Raif finds himself the prisoner as Ann tempts him like no one else.

A GOLDEN BETRAYAL

Available December 2012 from Harlequin® Desire.

HARLEQUIN *Presents*

When legacy commands, these Greek royals must obey!

Discover a page-turning new Harlequin Presents®
duet from *USA TODAY* bestselling author

Maisey Yates

A ROYAL WORLD APART

Desperate to escape an arranged marriage, Princess
Evangelina has tried every trick in her little black book
to dodge her security guards. But where everyone else
has failed, will her new bodyguard bend her to his
will…and steal her heart?

Available November 13, 2012.

AT HIS MAJESTY'S REQUEST

Prince Stavros Drakos rules his country like his
business—with a will of iron! And when duty demands
an heir, this resolute bachelor will turn his sole
focus to the task….

But will he finally have met his match in a world-
renowned matchmaker?

**Coming December 18, 2012,
wherever books are sold.**